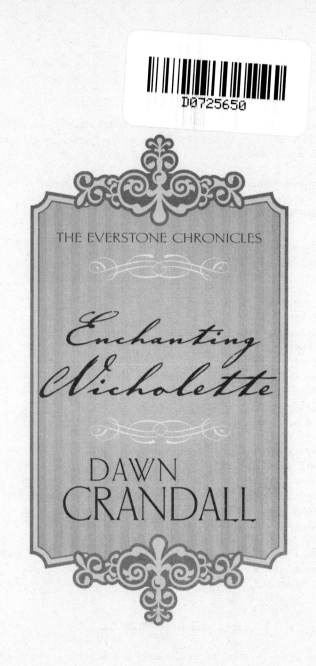

THE EVERSTONE CHRONICLES

Enchanting Nicholette

DAWN CRANDALL

WHITAKER
HOUSE

ENCHANTING NICHOLETTE

www.dawncrandall.blogspot.com
www.facebook.com/DawnCrandallWritesFirst
twitter.com/dawnwritesfirst

ISBN: 978-1-64123-088-9
eBook ISBN: 978-1-64123-089-6
Printed in the United States of America
© 2018 by Dawn Crandall

Whitaker House
1030 Hunt Valley Circle
New Kensington, PA 15068
www.whitakerhouse.com

Library of Congress Cataloguing-in-Publication Data
Names: Crandall, Dawn, 1977- author.
Title: Enchanting Nicholette / Dawn Crandall.
Description: New Kensington, PA : Whitaker House, [2018] | Series: The
   everstone chronicles ; 5 |
Identifiers: LCCN 2018030227 (print) | LCCN 2018031720 (ebook) | ISBN
   9781641230896 (e-book) | ISBN 9781641230889 (paperback)
Subjects: | BISAC: FICTION / Christian / Romance. | FICTION / Christian /
   Historical. | GSAFD: Christian fiction. | Love stories.
Classification: LCC PS3603.R3743 (ebook) | LCC PS3603.R3743 E56 2018
   (print)
   | DDC 813/.6—dc23
LC record available at https://lccn.loc.gov/2018030227

1 2 3 4 5 6 7 8 9 10 11 ⨄ 25 24 23 22 21 20 19 18

1

The Bookshop

"It was in looking up at him her aspect had caught its lustre—
the light repeated in her eyes beamed first out of his."
—Charlotte Brontë, *Villette*

Saturday, June 3, 1893 · Boston, Massachusetts

I suppose you have a new wardrobe ordered from Paris, *oui?*"

I glanced at the girl sitting across from me in my carriage
as we drove up the street toward Brittle Brattle Books, wondering,
for the life of me, how I'd come to the point of being so terribly
desperate for company.

My carriage companion, Sylvie Boutilier, was the youngest
daughter of my father-in-law's second wife, whom he'd married
the previous summer. Because we were of a similar age, I ended
up being the one who had the privilege of keeping her with me on
almost a daily basis.

Not that she was annoying, just so very naive. And fanciful.

In truth, she was unlike me in every way.

She continued, regardless of my silence. "Has it been delivered
yet?"

"Yes, it's been delivered." Though I couldn't fathom feeling the same wearing my normal, colorful gowns as I had before William had died. The big day was quickly approaching; the cards announcing my reentrance to society were all enveloped, stamped, and ready to send in the mail. Everything had been done weeks before, which gave me the feeling that my mourning period had been as difficult for my mother as it had been for me—though I had a feeling she quite enjoyed traveling through Europe for the last two years.

"I'm so pleased that you're back now, for it seems there aren't many young people my age in my stepfather's circle anymore. *Monsieur* Garrett Summercourt and his wife are *très merveilleux*, but they are married. And his brothers, *Monsieur* Alex and *Monsieur* Clyde...one is a snob and one is affianced." Sylvie touched my arm with her gloved fingertips. "At least I have you. We will help each other find husbands, *non?*"

I didn't answer. I wondered if Sylvie knew how my marriage had ended—too soon, my husband ripped away with one horrifically mistaken gunshot. I doubted it, but I couldn't bring myself to ask. My whole life had fallen apart two years ago, and I didn't know how to put it back together. Nor did I know how to request anyone's help in doing so.

Uncertainties constantly bombarded me, overwhelmed me on a daily basis. I was twenty-two, a widow of two years, my mourning almost complete, and I would soon be reentered into the only society I'd ever known—but as a new person.

Mrs. William Everstone, but without William.

He had loved me. Quite adamantly, in fact. So much so that it had been him who'd requested of my father that I marry him instead of his brother Nathan. There was so much more to it, but ultimately, it had been a favorable switch...that is, until the tragedy. Now Nathan was married to his beloved Amaryllis, and I was all alone again.

"You'll probably be married again, Nicholette, before I am," Sylvie added.

"I doubt that," I stated flatly. Although the idea of remarriage was something I'd contemplated for months already, I was certain my mother would faint at the mere thought. And really, who would I marry now? I'd grown up much in the last two lonely years, and I wasn't sure what I wanted anymore. Nor how to go about maneuvering the marriage market I had a feeling I would be thrown into soon enough.

"Your look is utterly *magnifique*. *Beaucoup plus belle* than I with my *cheveux roux*." She poked aggressively at the loosened strands of dark auburn hair slipping out from under her bonnet, as if her hair wasn't gorgeous. As if she wasn't gorgeous.

At times, I didn't even know what to say to her.

"The Summercourt brothers you just mentioned all have red hair," I attempted.

"Ah, *oui*, but they are men."

I didn't see her point, or the point of going on, so I let the subject end there. She went on to ask, "Do you know whom you would like to marry?"

"Um, no." I could feel the tension in my brow increase. I wanted so badly to frown, but I refrained. "How would I?"

"Surely if you've had your eye on someone, you could make them want to marry you. Isn't that how it's done?"

"Not in my experience."

No one I'd ever met had been able to turn my head enough to induce thoughts of going against my parents' wish for me to marry into the Everstone family. It was what I'd always known would happen…and I'd been quite agreeable to it.

And now what was I supposed to do? The thought of finagling my way through a sea of highly interested prospective suitors made me feel ill. I honestly didn't know what I would do if I met someone who interested me. I had absolutely no practice in flirting. Only following directions.

I took another quick glance at Sylvie.

She was sixteen—six years younger than me—and she seemed to have such a natural allure, but in a rather likable way. She was so approachable and candid, two terms that would never describe me in a hundred years.

The carriage slowed to a smooth stop, and I looked outside to see the large golden lettering backed by dark green over the multipaned storefront windows of Brittle Brattle Books.

Sylvie scooted toward the door, which was opened by the groom.

"A few minutes, please, Lamont." I reached for the handle, closing the door again. "Sylvie, I have a request to make of you, and I hope you won't find it offensive—"

"Oh, I don't think I would! You can ask me anything."

My gaze lingered at the carriage door again, and I bit my lip. Perhaps it was too silly of a thing to ask. What would she think of me? But then she had assumed I would likely be remarried before she married at all. So of course she would want to help me…right? And it wasn't as if I were asking her to help me secure a husband; I just wanted to feel more comfortable.

More prepared.

"What is it?" Sylvie asked, her eyes wide in anticipation.

What on earth did she think I was going to ask? Nothing too shocking, I hoped. She hardly knew me, after all. She wouldn't have known that I was the least shocking person in all of Back Bay.

"About my getting married again someday…." I looked up to see her reaction to my words. She was smiling, almost giddily. "You see, I might need some help with that."

"You want me to help? Whom do you want to marry? I can't wait to meet him!"

"Um, no, I don't—I don't know him." I almost wanted to forget about my request…but then I thought about living with my parents for years and years and not ever again having the kind of connection that had begun between William and me. And who better was there to ask than Sylvie, whom I'd seen flirt quite effortlessly a number of times since I'd met her?

"I would like your help in knowing what I'm supposed to do regarding men."

"You are…oh, what's the word? Careful?"

"I've always been quite the opposite of encouraging."

"Hmm, perhaps I should study how you do," Sylvie said, with her finger to her lips.

"I'm afraid you will be sorely disappointed in my lack of skills."

"You aren't *superflu*, but that's not terrible." Sylvie scooted toward the door and reached for the handle. "*Zut alors!* What if he's inside this bookshop? What will you do?" She said this remark as she made her way out of the carriage and then waited for me to follow.

"What if who is inside?" I asked as I descended the small metal steps down to the sidewalk.

"Your *him*." She gasped happily, looping her arm with mine.

Him.

The sudden thought thrilled me, probably more than it should have. I did want to marry again someday, to find someone who not only loved me, but understood me in ways that William never had.

Was that why I hadn't fallen in love with him? Perhaps I'd not had enough time. Perhaps falling in love was a long process. Maybe it took longer than the time I'd been given. And perhaps actually having a marriage beyond my tragic wedding day would have helped.

Sylvie squeezed my arm. "Don't be shy about wanting to marry again—that is lesson one. No one will blame you, believe me."

I didn't outwardly respond right away to Sylvie's first lesson as we walked down the sidewalk toward Brittle Brattle Books, but her words had a profound impact on my heart. Not that I was intent on finding a new husband that day, but I'd always been wary of showing an interest in men for fear that they would pursue me. Because I hadn't wanted them to. But now…how was I supposed to switch that part of my thinking around?

"I will try my best, Sylvie."

God, I have no idea what I'm doing. Please help.

As Sylvie opened the door deeply set in the windowed front, the bells hanging off the inside door handle clanged loudly, announcing our arrival. Before going in, I noticed a display of books inside the front window to our right. A copy of my sister-in-law's book, *The Little Fox*—the only one published so far—was situated with a number of other little books that also looked like they were written for children.

"Oh, I do hope they have more than one!" Sylvie gripped my arm tighter, and then pulled me through the open door.

"I'm sure they wouldn't put their only copy in the window display, Sylvie," I said as she guided me toward the cashier's counter, where a tall, slender gentleman stood sorting through a pile of books. When we drew near to him, he took a moment to look up, and then asked, "May I be of service, ladies?"

"We are looking for a copy—actually quite a few copies—of a book you have in your front window. The one called *The Little Fox* by Violet Hawthorne."

"We have a number of copies of that one. Written by one of our own, you know. The author lives right here in Boston. Married to one of those Everstone gents now, but I believe she was from Maine originally."

"Yes, we know," I stated. "Will you please point us in the direction of the books?"

"Should be right there near the far corner." He motioned toward the back of the large double-leveled room in which we were standing.

Shocked that he hadn't felt the need to actually find the books for us, I stood there for a moment longer, then turned to Sylvie. "I suppose they shouldn't be too difficult to find."

She was already on her way to the other end of the large room when the bells at the front door rang again, announcing another customer.

I glanced over my shoulder and noticed a fairly tall, well-built gentleman with sandy brown hair sticking out from the sides of his silk top hat held the door for an elegant, well-dressed young lady. He laughed softly, with a hint of a smile on his lips, as he said something to her.

I felt something odd, what seemed like an almost-memory. Whatever it was, it was something I'd never felt before, and it lit a fire in my chest and stole the breath from my lungs.

Which was ridiculous. How could so many strange sensations be the result of catching one glimpse of a man? And even if I was attracted by the outward appearance of this stranger, the chance that I'd ever see him again was highly unlikely.

I dared another glance. Had I met this man before? He seemed to be relatively familiar, perhaps from many years past. But I couldn't place him, no matter how I tried.

Tearing my gaze from the two of them before either he or the young lady with him caught me staring, I followed Sylvie to the back of the store. However, after a few steps, I couldn't help but look back, very subtly, over my shoulder. The two of them were now separated—she at the counter speaking to the bookseller, and he… where had he gone? I faced forward for a moment and then turned to look over my other shoulder. I found him standing against the bookcase along the wall parallel to where the cashier's counter was situated. He was holding open a periodical, but watching me.

His eyes locked with mine, and he had that same hint of a smile on his face I'd seen a few minutes before. His eyes were a dark, grayish-blue, and they stayed on me, awaiting my response, as if no one else in the room mattered.

Would I respond? What was the response needed? A smile back? A nod? I was too flustered to know, so I faced the back of the store again, suddenly heated and breathless.

My only intent now, as I made my way to the corner where Sylvie waited, was to pretend that he wasn't alive. No matter who he was, I shouldn't have let him see that I'd been looking for him after I'd already decided it was a bad idea to stare. What had I been thinking to linger, as if I couldn't get enough of the sight of a mere stranger? And while still wearing a half-mourning gown!

I found Sylvie staring earnestly at a bookshelf, her gaze traveling down one row of books, and then the next.

"I thought you did not know how to flirt," she said softly, her accent making her words sound almost like a purr.

"I don't even know him," I whispered with as much emphasis as I could allow.

"Maybe you should. Perhaps it is he who you were to meet in the bookshop today."

"Ladies and gentlemen aren't introduced in bookshops. And how would we know he is a gentleman? He could be anyone."

"Ah, but he could also be *him*."

"This is the silliest conversation I've ever had. Please stop. Let's look for the books you came in here for." I scanned the rows of books, wishing the man at the cashier's counter had felt the inclination to help us in the first place. Then nothing of the last five minutes would have happened, and I wouldn't have to pretend the gentleman on the other side of the room didn't exist.

Not that I'd likely forget him anytime soon.

"Here!" Sylvie finally announced. She held up only one copy of the long-sought-after book. "There is but one."

"Surely there are more than that. The bookseller said there were a number of them." I continued to search the shelves, my gaze roving back and forth over the spines of hundreds of books, hoping they were simply misplaced and we wouldn't have to go through the lengthy process of special ordering them with the help of the man at the front counter. I wanted to get the books and leave. Quickly.

Although I hadn't looked to the front end of the store since catching his eye, I felt the attractive stranger's gaze on me still. Was he standing near the periodicals? Or was he helping his companion look for the book she'd come in to find? Heat flushed my neck again, remembering how bold I'd been to so obviously look for him. And I felt as if I'd entertained him in my absurd endeavor to study him.

I didn't like the feelings the situation had created…the uncertainty of what was going on…the thrilling feeling that something *could* happen.

"I found them!" Sylvie exclaimed happily while she used one finger under her chin to subtly point to the shelves above the ones we'd been scanning. "But they are up there."

Sure enough, about a dozen copies of the tiny book rested on a shelf well beyond our reach. Beside us, a tall, narrow ladder hung from a track on the high ceiling.

Wanting only to leave the bookshop and Mr. Hinted Smile's presence as quickly as possible, I didn't think twice about not asking the man at the counter for help. It would take much too long, plus I'd risk walking past *him* and his companion.

Twisting my reticule to the other side of my wrist, I grabbed the small rungs of the ladder and started up the few short steps to reach the books. Sylvie wanted three more, and since they were very small, I was pretty sure I'd be able to grab them all in one swift move and make my way back down in short time. But that was not taking into account the heels of my boots.

As I slipped my fingers around a number of the books and went to maneuver them off the shelf, I lost my balance and wobbled. And then, because my heels were caught on the rungs, I fell back and quite literally, straight off the ladder.

I closed my eyes, my arms extended into the air above me, quite unladylike, and then waited for a drastic landing onto the hard, wooden floor below.

But instead, I found myself in a pair of strong arms.

Since my eyes were still closed, and I clutched the only book left in my hands—after losing the others—I prayed silently and fervently that the arms were those of the gangly bookseller....

But I knew better.

I knew exactly whose arms they were.

2

Introductions

"You don't need scores of suitors.
You need only one...*if he's the right one.*"
—Louisa May Alcott, *Little Women*

W
hy, this is just what I was looking for," came a strong male voice that matched the arms holding me.

I opened my eyes, and yes, it was indeed *him*.

"Someone to fall into your arms?" Sylvie asked from behind me.

Before anyone answered her silly question, I was placed upon my feet, no worse for the wear, except that my pride had taken quite a beating ever since walking into Brittle Brattle Books.

I handed the book still in my hands to Sylvie. "Here you are."

The gentleman went about gathering my reticule and the books I'd dropped. Handing one book to Sylvie, he said, "Rescuing a falling beauty from spilling to the floor wasn't exactly what I was looking for, *mademoiselle*"—picking up on Sylvie's French accent—"but it was an added pleasure, let me assure you." He then turned to me, handing me my reticule. "You are all right, I hope? I headed over as soon as I realized your intent—"

"Yes, I'm fine. I'm not sure what induced me to do such a thing." I glanced up at his face for the first time since he'd retrieved the books from the floor. He was smiling now, fully, and I noticed he had a dimple on each cheek. It made him look impossibly attractive—and quite boyish—though he was surely well into his twenties.

"I'm glad I was around," he said, catching my eye, quite on purpose.

"What is it you were looking for exactly?" I asked, ignoring his implications. Yes, he was handsome, but I didn't know the first thing about him, and I had now made a complete fool of myself in front of him—because of him—and it was all such a horrendous mistake to have come. We should have simply stayed home and sent a servant to run our errand.

"Why, that—"

At that moment, both the bookseller and the young lady this fascinating man had come into the store with came up beside us.

"I do hope you haven't hurt yourself for the sake of a book, ma'am. I should have been the one to get that down for you."

"Or at the very least, you could have asked me," my rescuer stated, giving me that half smile yet again.

I didn't want to go into the reasoning behind my thoughtless adventure up the ladder for the bookseller, so I simply responded, "I'm not hurt. I'm perfectly fine thanks to..." But then I realized my mistake. It seemed I was practically begging for an introduction.

Which I wasn't.

And had he been teasing me? Because I'd gawked at him in a very unladylike manner when he'd come into the store behind us?

Probably.

But really, sometimes one's eyes had no way of turning away, as I was quickly learning.

"Oh, Cal, you found the book," the girl said. Now that I saw her up close, she had to be about the same age as Sylvie. And she had to be his sister, or possibly his cousin. The resemblance between them was astounding. She had the same sandy, light-brown hair and dark-gray eyes, and their faces were so similar. I looked between them again, despite knowing it was a bad idea. He had such a good shape to his face, such good cheekbones, and that subtle smile.

I forced myself to look away now. What was wrong with me? I'd never in my life had such a difficult time not looking at a man, and I'd been loved by one of the handsomest men I'd ever known.

He held up the copy of *The Little Fox.* "We came in here looking for a copy of this book," he said, finally getting around to answering the one question I had asked of him.

"Really? This book?" I asked, taking it from his hand. I didn't believe him.

"Yes, this book." He took it back, playfully. "We came in here with the sole aim of purchasing a copy. We happen to know the author quite well."

"We know the author, too! Well, almost," Sylvie burst in, pleased with herself. "We're both related to her through marriage—"

"You're both connected to our cousin Violet through the Everstone family?" the girl beside Sylvie asked. "That's brilliant!"

The girl's unexpected response shocked me into a most-euphoric sensation as I realized this man was my own sister-in-law's cousin, Cal Hawthorne. I'd heard mention of Violet's cousins many times in the last weeks. I would have eventually been properly introduced to him and likely often associated with him by way of the Everstones, regardless of my foolishness in the bookshop.

Of course, here I had this as our introduction. Now, that was just brilliant.

Mr. Hawthorne's voice broke through my thoughts, "You are the former Miss Nicholette Fairbanks, now Mrs. William Everstone."

I looked him square in the face at this admission, unabashedly, trying to place him. Had I met him before? Wouldn't I have remembered his face? He had such a way about him that had captured my attention despite my better judgment. But then again, I hadn't been interested in taking much notice of the gentlemen around me before. I'd been patiently resigned to do as my parents wanted, which hadn't been a bad thing.

I noticed now, however. Oh, and how I noticed.

But if Mr. Hawthorne knew of me, did he happen to recall exactly how long William and I had been married? How William had been murdered on our wedding day? It wasn't shameful to have been married and widowed so early, and so young, but that didn't stop my continual embarrassment whenever I knew the subject was under consideration.

Sylvie and Mr. Hawthorne's sister, presumably, now stood a few feet away, busy studying Violet's beautiful illustrations in *The Little Fox*, so I went on speaking entirely to him.

"May I then have the pleasure of an introduction, Mr. Hawthorne?" I dared to ask with the faintest of whispers, looking him in the eye and giving away that I, too, already knew who he was.

He looked at me as if he were trying to figure something out, for whatever reason. "You may have the pleasure." He bowed minutely. "As my sister said, Violet is our cousin, and I am Mr. Hawthorne, Mr. Cal Hawthorne." Lifting his eyes, yet again, to meet mine, he continued, "Mrs. Everstone, this is my sister, Miss Mabel Hawthorne. Mabel, meet Mrs. Nicholette Everstone... and...?"

"I'm so happy to make your acquaintance, Mrs. Everstone. Please, you both must call me Mabel. I have a feeling we'll be seeing a lot more of each other after this, since we are connected through Violet."

Mabel then looked expectantly at Sylvie, whom she'd already been speaking to exclusively for a number of minutes. It was such a strange way of being introduced—all on our own without the benefit of having our shared acquaintance there.

"This," I said, "is my father-in-law Bram Everstone's step-daughter, Miss Sylvie Boutilier—recently arrived from France, having completed finishing school."

"A pleasure, Miss Boutilier." Mr. Hawthorne smiled, but this time, entirely for Sylvie.

I'd never been one to get jealous easily—well, not usually—but I had to wonder if Mr. Hawthorne had heard me say that Sylvie had recently graduated finishing school? But perhaps he liked her easy, open manner, and the fact that she was young and her heart unscathed.

"The pleasure is returned, let me assure you. And do feel free to use my name…Sylvie," she said, her French accent adding to her already overabundant allure. She took Mabel's hand, and then Mr. Hawthorne's.

"May we call you Cal since we have the honor of such close relations?" Sylvie asked.

"Sylvie, you shouldn't ask—"

He gave me the slightest of bows, providing his consent as he said, "Yes, you may all call me Cal."

"Mrs. Everstone," Mabel started awkwardly, since I'd been the only one of the small group who hadn't given permission to use my Christian name, "I'm sorry to hear of your loss. I had heard of the tragedy while first getting to know your extended family a year ago. The Everstones truly are a beautiful family. I'm sure you were pleased to have married into such a wonderful group of people."

"Thank you," I said, quickly turning away from Mr. Hawthorne, trying desperately not to lose my well-practiced composure at the mention of my marriage. But when Sylvie and Mabel seemed to—quite purposefully—turn and walk together to the front of the bookshop, I took the opportunity to ask, "Have we met before, Mr. Hawthorne?"

"We've never been properly introduced, no, but I did know who you were as Miss Nicholette Fairbanks. We've been in mixed company a number of times in past years."

"That's so very odd, for I don't recall you at all." I glanced up, unable to resist sharing my next thoughts. "I think I would, to be honest."

"Your honestly is greatly appreciated, Mrs. Everstone." Again, the sight of those dimples and his smile made my stomach flutter.

"I have to admit, at first glance, I didn't recognize you. I certainly didn't expect it to be you, back from your travels."

"If we've been in mixed company a number of times, why were we never introduced?"

"I would have requested an introduction, but I didn't think it prudent, considering you were spoken for...and my whole goal in being introduced would have been to court you."

I swallowed, and I could hear my heartbeat pound in my ears. "Indeed?"

"Indeed," was his only reply.

"How long ago was this? Where?" I asked. I felt as if I were prying, but he'd been agreeable to the conversation from the beginning, and I was merely going along...no matter how personal, no matter how the whole exchange produced the feeling of having a dozen butterflies in my stomach.

"Four years ago, perhaps, here in Boston. You were very young, just out."

The flusters intensified, and I could barely speak. When they finally settled, I was able to say, "My, you have an excellent memory."

He shrugged. "I must admit, you left a profound impression upon me."

"Oh, I see," I attempted, stunned by his frankness.

He went on thoughtfully, "Though, back then I thought you were to marry the eldest Everstone brother, Nathan Everstone."

"That didn't work out so well," I said, slowly getting acclimated to the open manner of our conversation. It was so very easy to speak with him, about almost everything. I'd never known anything like it, except for how close I'd become to William during our engagement. But even that was different. We were supposed to talk about everything.

This, with Mr. Cal Hawthorne now, was happening entirely because I wanted to know more about him. And he obviously wanted to know more of me as well, having even admitted the desire to court me at one time.

"Nathan fell in love with someone else, and as it turned out, William had long harbored affection for me. Not that marrying William wasn't what I wanted at the time we were engaged. I had looked forward to—"

Good grief, what was I saying? Was this my best effort at being flirtatious—talking about how much I'd looked forward to marrying my first husband?

"I'm sorry." I fidgeted with the binding of Violet's book. "I shouldn't have said that."

"That you wanted to marry your fiancé? Please, I'm glad he had the fortune of possessing your heart. He was an extremely lucky man. It's what we all wish to find in marriage, is it not?"

"Yes, it is," I admitted, sadly.

"You wouldn't know, but I, too, have been married before. My wife passed away almost five years ago." He let out a long breath, as if saying so affected him physically. I could easily imagine the sense of loss, grief, and past sorrow such words could produce.

At this admission, I realized the reason I'd felt such a curious connection to him. He knew exactly how I felt. Though we'd just met, he knew parts of me that even my closest family and friends couldn't understand.

"Alice passed away three months after we were married. She'd been unwell for some time, but still, it was unexpected."

Alice.

It felt ridiculous to even think such things, but I immediately wondered if he missed belonging to someone as much as I did. But why hadn't he married again after so many years? Surely he would have if he'd wanted to. Surely, he could have chosen to marry anyone he wanted. Anyone.

"I'm sorry." I didn't know what else to say, and suddenly, I reheard all of the similar comments I'd received in the last two years with new ears. I realized how awkward it felt to find something worth saying in such a situation.

"It's quite all right. Coming from you, it means a great deal."

Yes, he understood completely. And suddenly, I had the strangest sensation that standing there with him, beside him, sharing such telling sentiments, was the most natural, perfect thing…and that he felt it, too.

"Well, we had better be going," Sylvie interrupted as she came up to us and grabbed my arm. I hadn't realized how close Mr. Hawthorne and I had been standing until she came between us. "We found exactly what we were looking for, and now we must be off to attend to our long list of errands."

Did Sylvie realize she was interrupting the most meaningful conversation I'd had in years?

"It was wonderful to meet the two of you," she went on. "I am sure we will have a chance to become acquainted once your cousin and her husband return to Boston from their vacation in Maine."

"It won't be long now." Mabel looped her arm through her brother's. "It was only a short visit to see her sister-in-law and the new baby. They will be back soon. And I'm certain we will see each other in the future. I will be counting the days, won't you, Cal?"

"Counting already, sister."

Finally, we excused ourselves, and Mr. Hawthorne went up the ladder to retrieve another copy of *The Little Fox* from the upper shelf. I led Sylvie to the counter with the books as well as the newest edition of *Harper's Bazaar* that she'd been looking forward to reading.

After paying for our purchases and leaving the store, Sylvie took my arm in hers again. "That was absolutely remarkable. Mr. Hawthorne had eyes only for you. You did notice, *non?* Are you not pleased?"

Pleased was a good word for it, but there was a part of me that felt unprepared for what my emotions were doing to me concerning this man. I didn't know how to answer her. I didn't know what to divulge, what to believe.

It wasn't the first time a man had noticed me, of course.

Just the first time I'd cared to notice him back.

3

Hawthorne House

"You never know what is enough
unless you know what is more than enough."
—William Blake, *The Marriage of Heaven and Hell*

Monday, June 19, 1893 · South Boston, Massachusetts

My mother's elderly friend, Miss Claudine Abernathy, had quite decided that Sylvie and I needed to meet Miss Mabel Hawthorne and her mother, whom she'd become dear friends with since Violet had married Vance Everstone. Thus, we found ourselves in Miss Abernathy's carriage, traveling to the Hawthornes' house.

Of course, Sylvie and I had never brought up our meeting Violet's cousins in the weeks since our visit to the bookshop. I hadn't known what to think, let alone what to say, about that day. However, I did know that Sylvie had been all too happy to have met Mabel and she was looking forward to seeing her new friend again. It hadn't seemed that she'd given Mr. Hawthorne a fleeting thought, which to me, was strange.

Had she not seen him?

Unfortunately, I had…and I couldn't get the thought of seeing him again out of my mind.

For as much as I'd tried not to think about—well, anything from that day—I simply couldn't help but admit that I'd enjoyed those few minutes of special attention from him in the bookshop. Even though, at the time, I'd been quite embarrassed, I found I desperately wanted him to continue those teasing ways.

I had a feeling that if he did, we would suit very well. And to tell the truth, from our limited time together, I knew I had come to like him far more than I'd allowed myself to like anyone ever before. I'd never had such a strange sensation—that I knew he would love me, if I wanted him to.

I sat next to Sylvie in Miss Abernathy's carriage, both of us facing her and her Pomeranian, Winston. I couldn't help but fiddle nervously with the strings of my reticule, wondering if I would perhaps see Mr. Hawthorne that very afternoon. We were almost there, and I hadn't yet had the courage to ask if Mabel Hawthorne's brother would possibly be in attendance.

When we were most of the way to South Boston, Sylvie leaned toward me a bit and whispered, "And now I will tell you lesson number two: be spontaneous. You need much help in this regard."

"I doubt Mr. Hawthorne will even be present." My words were barely audible, in case Miss Abernathy's hearing was, by chance, better than she let on.

"It's interesting that you should bring him up," Sylvie continued softly, her face forward, her chin up, and eyes focused on the window at her side of the carriage. "I hope he is, for I believe there is a high chance you could make him fall madly in love with you, quite easily."

"Sylvie, please."

She slid a narrow glance my way, tipping her lips into a sly grin. "But you want him, *non?*"

I didn't even bother to answer. It would have been much too difficult without lying. Instead, I said, "Sylvie, I do want to be married again someday, yes. But I don't know who I should marry at this precise moment." I looked out the window, hoping she wouldn't read anything of my thoughts from the blush I felt creeping up my neck. "I'm quite certain Mr. Hawthorne hasn't had the first thought about me regarding such things."

"I would not say so. Mabel says he hasn't paid mind to any woman in years. At least not the way he did the day he met you."

"When did she say this? Have you seen her since that day?"

"*Non*! It was while you were talking with *Monsieur* Hawthorne at the bookshop. I noticed then, he had eyes only for you."

"Really, Sylvie, I'm quite certain Mr. Hawthorne doesn't need your help."

"Ooh, yes? Why do you say that? What was said?"

"Nothing."

"That nothing does not sound like a nothing. Tell me. You seemed to have quite a lot to say to one another that day, for just having met."

Miss Abernathy pounded the end of her cane on the floor of the carriage, startling the small dog in her lap and waking him. "What are you two whispering about over there?"

"We were wondering about Mr. Hawthorne," Sylvie admitted happily.

Too happily in my opinion. She really needed to learn more about the art of subtleness. But then, I supposed that would have ruined her open, ready manner that everyone seemed to like so much.

"Ah, Mr. Hawthorne. I had a feeling you two might have an interest in meeting that particular young man."

"Oh, not for me," Sylvie replied. "But perhaps Nicholette will like him well enough."

"I'm not...but I'm not...." *In the market for a husband,* was what I'd wanted to say, but the words lodged in my throat as the lie they were. Not just any husband, no. But I couldn't deny that I had my hopes about Mr. Cal Hawthorne.

"And as you should, Nicholette," Miss Abernathy admonished, ignoring my feeble attempt at turning the conversation some- where—anywhere—else. Sylvie seemed to have a special knack for bringing up awkward conversations, and she took immense delight in making me participate in them.

"If I were but forty years younger," Miss Abernathy sighed. Then she brought her gaze back to me and asked pointedly, "Are you ready for another husband, Nicholette?"

"I—I hardly know. I never had one in the first place."

"How sadly true. But you know what? This time, you don't have to do what your mother feels is best. This time, I have on good authority from your father that you may marry whomever you like, as long as it's for love."

"Yes, I suppose. Within reason, at least."

"Well, I'm quite certain you'll find Mr. Hawthorne *within reason*, and quite amiable. His mother has told me he has been a bit of a recluse since he'd been widowed, not paying much mind to the young ladies who, I'm sure, are very interested in gaining his attention."

He had seemed like the kind of man who could attract the attention of any woman, no matter her tastes. He was handsome and likable, with a charming personality. I'd never been drawn to someone so completely, as I had been to him.

"His marriage, you see, was arranged much the same way yours to William had been, dear, put about by his father. But then his wife died shortly afterwards...well, now he seems to have found himself in quite the same place as you have. You're both in the position to marry whomever you please this time. Isn't that, well, doesn't that seem providential?"

"Quite," Sylvie supplied for me.

"And what do you think about all this, Nicholette?"

"He's a relatively young widower, you say?" I asked, hoping and praying that my subterfuge wouldn't be discovered by the end of the afternoon.

That seemed to be enough encouragement, for Miss Abernathy went on. "Nicholette, I know you're apt to be shy and that you come across a bit harsh at times because of it...but you must try. No one is going to hand you a husband like William Everstone on a silver platter this time."

"Yes, ma'am." It was about all I could muster, as I was quite surprised to hear a lecture about allowing myself to fall for a certain Mr. Cal Hawthorne. Little did she know that she could save her breath, because I was already halfway there.

But I couldn't very well tell her that. I wouldn't have, even if she'd known about our previous meeting. Instead of trying to deny or explain or make any kind of excuse, I decided then and there that it would be a lovely gesture to let her believe everything I'd already experienced between myself and Mr. Hawthorne came about because of her fervent prayers.

"I doubt he'll be there this afternoon, but you'll meet his mother and his sister. I've told them both all about you, and they look forward to this visit. Mabel especially, I think. Her mother is a sweet woman who has become very dear to me in the last year, and I'm sure you two will adore Mabel. She has been a great friend and help to Violet as she's acclimated to living in Boston. She isn't fully out yet, like you, Sylvie, but perhaps you will both debut this autumn. Surely your mother has plans regarding that."

"Ah, *oui*. And wouldn't it be *magnifique* to involve Miss Hawthorne!"

At this point in our conversation, the carriage turned onto a small street off Fourth Street, which had taken us all the way to

South Boston, and parked on the side of the street, next to a large oak tree.

"Here they are." Miss Abernathy motioned toward a newly built side-by-side Federal style townhouse with wood siding, black shutters, and two matching double doors that practically shared a front porch. "Letty and Mabel live in the townhouse to the right, while Mr. Hawthorne lives on his own in the townhouse to the left. But he has his meals with them, of course."

It was such a strange setup, and not at all the kind of house I imagined they would live in. Though it was a good neighborhood, and the houses were newly built and nice, I thought...I thought Mr. Hawthorne would live in a bigger, or better situated house. I'd imagined something more like the estates my family and our closest friends owned in Back Bay.

This was just two adjoined townhouses.

"I know it doesn't look like much, dear. But Letty wanted a quiet life here in South Boston, opposed to the way they used to live in Westborough before her husband died. Our young Mr. Hawthorne had attended Harvard, you see, and had already settled here in Boston. Though I think Letty said he and his wife lived near Back Bay for the short time they were married. It made sense, when both her husband and daughter-in-law had passed away, that the family would find a house where they could all live together, but separately."

"He went from living near Back Bay to G Street in South Boston...on purpose?" I hoped I didn't sound as incredulous as I felt.

"Nicholette, dear, not everyone who happens to have the money to flaunt has the desire to do so. As I said, they like the quiet life. They like to be left alone. Which I suppose is precisely why Letty has it in her head to move to Everston."

I'd been to Everston for Estella Everstone's wedding to Dexter Blakeley. It was a resort in the middle of the sprawling green mountains of central Maine that William's sister and her husband owned. Perhaps it was the fact that Everston was to be her future that they lived as modestly as they did now. It would cost a fortune to have his mother situated at Everston for the rest of her days.

Which twisted my thoughts in another direction. "Is the entire family moving to Maine?"

"No, not the family, and really, I highly doubt anything will come of Letty's wishful plans. For one, I know her children wouldn't want her to live apart from them. And secondly, I have it on good authority that Letty and Mabel will likely move to Everthorne to live with Violet and Vance before all is said and done. And Mr. Hawthorne…well, I guess I never did figure out what his plans were. Hopefully they consist of marrying again and settling down here in Boston."

I sucked in my breath a little too quickly as I descended the metal steps onto the sidewalk. I could just imagine.

"I could see him doing that," Sylvie said as she climbed out of the carriage behind me.

"And I've been thinking." Miss Abernathy stood before us, holding her fluffy dog in one arm, and tapping the end of her cane—which I didn't believe she needed—against an oak tree. "Retiring to a place like Everston, and being near to Estella and Dexter and baby Gracie. Even if Letty wasn't able to come—which I can't see her doing—it does all sound quite delightful."

"You mean, you would consider retiring to Everston?" I asked. "Whatever would you do with Hilldreth Manor?"

"Nathan and Amaryllis actually own the house. It was part of her inheritance. But they're never going to live there. I would be surprised if they came back east for years to come now that they have little ones. It's much too difficult to get from Washington to Boston with children, even with the private railcar. I suppose they will sell it."

"Sell Hilldreth Manor?" The thought of Miss Abernathy not living in the Victorian brick mansion on the corner of Commonwealth Avenue and Berkeley Street was appalling. It had been one of those houses I'd practically grown up in, given that Claudine Abernathy was so central to the world of people I knew. It would be like Bram Everstone deciding to sell Everwood, or my parents selling Faircourt. If Miss Claudine Abernathy moved away from Boston, nothing would ever be the same.

Having such world-altering thoughts stream through my mind as I walked up to the Hawthornes' very unconventional house was not how I'd pictured presenting myself to Mr. Hawthorne's mother. Sylvie came up beside me and looped her arm through mine. "Maybe you should buy Hilldreth Manor."

"Me? What would I...?" But then the thought of the independence from my parents I'd been robbed of when William was accidentally murdered came to me, and I pictured myself coming and going from Hilldreth Manor whenever I chose, decorating those wonderful high-ceilinged rooms with my favorite pieces of art, my own furniture. Everything I'd never had the chance to do with Fairstone.

And being married again.

But this time, *really* married.

For love, and for longer than a day.

Sylvie and I quietly followed Miss Abernathy up the steps to the right side of the shared porch. Before we were even at the door, it swung open to reveal Mabel Hawthorne in the entryway, smiling and literally bouncing with excitement.

Before anyone could say a thing about meeting already, Miss Abernathy took it upon herself to start the introductions. "Sylvie, Nicholette, this is Miss Mabel Hawthorne, my friend's daughter. Mabel, this is Mrs. Nicholette Everstone and Miss Sylvie Boutilier."

"It's so gloriously wonderful to finally meet you!" Mabel said, pretending to meet us for the first time. She took Sylvie's arm, detaching her from my clutch, and propelled her through the wide hall past the tall, straight staircase to our left, and then through the large opening into the parlor.

The Hawthornes' maid silently closed the door behind us, then took our things and hung them on the hooks next to a giant mirror on the wall. "Miss Abernathy, Mrs. Hawthorne will be down momentarily."

As I walked into the parlor behind everyone, I took note of the excellent embellishments and furnishings, which were clearly put together by a professional. These rooms were what I expected from everything I'd heard about the Hawthornes. But it was strange they would live so extravagantly inside. No one walking by would ever guess the inside of 55 G Street looked as it did.

We were seated in the parlor. Miss Abernathy, holding Winston, sat in an armchair near one end of the sofa on which Sylvie, Mabel, and I sat. Mrs. Hawthorne came down the staircase, accompanied by her maid.

When they finally reached the entrance to the parlor, Mrs. Hawthorne said, "I'm sorry, I wasn't feeling all that well. I was resting, but please do stay. I've so looked forward to this visit." The maid virtually held her in a standing position until she gently guided her to the chair situated at the opposite end of the sofa.

No one had ever revealed that Mr. Hawthorne's mother was ill, but it was clear to me without an explanation now. Her face, neck, and hands all had a chalky hue, which looked rather ghastly in comparison to her high-collared black shirtwaist, and her green eyes had a sunken look to them. Although she was probably near the same age as my mother, she seemed much, much older...and frail. She honestly looked as if she might not make it another few years. It was no wonder her children didn't want her to move to Everston. They likely would never see her again. And why would she want to leave her children?

Unless she thought they would follow....

"Letty, let me introduce you to the young ladies I've told you all about. Mrs. Nicholette Everstone"—she indicated me—"I've known her parents most of her life, and I can tell you, there aren't better people in the world."

Since we were seated, and Mrs. Hawthorne looked completely drained from making her way down the stairs, we did nothing more than nod to one another as introductions were made.

"And this is Miss Sylvie Boutilier," Miss Abernathy continued. "She's Bram Everstone's new wife's youngest daughter, and she's just completed finishing school in Paris in May and come to live with them. The rest of Evangeline's children from her first marriage are married and still live in France, of course."

"Nicholette, Sylvie, this my dearest friend, Mrs. Letty Hawthorne, of Westborough, Massachusetts."

"It's nice to meet you, Mrs. Hawthorne," I said. "I've heard much about your family since coming home from Europe last month."

"Yes, and I've heard about your family for well over a year now. Your old friends have been quite eager for your return. I suppose your mourning period is recently ended?"

"Yes, at the beginning of June."

"I fear my own mourning will never end," she said, not really looking at any of us.

"Now, Letty, you have a good many things to focus on without thinking only of your Robert. Your son and daughter, I can say with all confidence, are two of the most accomplished and amiable young people I've ever met...and they love you."

"Yes, I know. I should think of them, and not him...."

Sylvie had yet to say much but only sat quietly beside me. Was she as surprised as I to find this half-stricken woman to be vibrant Miss Abernathy's best friend?

Mrs. Hawthorne smiled, in a pained sort of way. "I'm sorry, I must apologize...perhaps I shouldn't have come out of my room." Another little dog, which matched Miss Abernathy's Winston to perfection, came running into the parlor from the hall, filling the room with chirpy barking. "Oh, Snowflake, do hush."

The dog went over to Miss Abernathy and continued to yap at Winston, which fortunately didn't feel the need to reciprocate.

Miss Abernathy pushed Winston off her lap and stood. "Well, then let's get you back to bed. There's no sense in our tiring you out if you feel you can't abide it." Her words seemed harsh, but as she went over to the bell pull to summon the maid and then helped Mrs. Hawthorne up from her seat—without her cane, I noticed— she did so with the utmost gentleness.

"I'm sorry I don't feel well, but you young ladies...please do stay and visit with my Mabel. Stay as long as you like. Please, don't mind me."

Once Miss Abernathy, Mrs. Hawthorne, and the maid were on their way up the stairs with the two tiny dogs following, Sylvie and I looked at one another, not knowing what to say or expect.

There could be no mother and daughter more opposite than Mrs. Hawthorne and Mabel.

And Mr. Hawthorne...where did he fit into the dynamic?

I wished I could have seen him with his mother; I would have loved to see how he reacted to his mother's frailty. I had a feeling he would've been more mindful of her than his younger sister. Mabel hadn't seemed to mind at all. She had seemed quite all right letting Miss Abernathy take care of her mother, instead of helping her herself.

But she was young. And perhaps, with such differing personalities, she just didn't know what to do. I could hardly blame her. I wasn't certain what I would have done in her situation.

Mabel leaned over a tad and said lowly, looking straight at me with a crooked grin, "Well, now we can get on with the real visit."

4

The Passage

"I won't say she was silly, but I think one of us was silly,
and it was not me."
—Elizabeth Gaskell, *Wives and Daughters*

This is great fun, isn't it?" Mabel asked. "Knowing one another already a bit, but everyone thinking we're new acquaintances? Well, except for Cal, of course, but he's not here."

"I was glad to keep it a secret," Sylvie admitted. "A fun secret, just between the four of us. And do tell, Mabel, why is your brother not here today? Did he not know we were to come?"

"He's extremely busy. It was rare enough he had time to go with me to Brittle Brattle Books that day, to tell the truth."

"How providential." Sylvie smirked at me, using Miss Abernathy's preferred word for the situation I'd found myself in.

"I wish a gentleman would catch me from falling off a ladder in a bookshop." Mabel sighed. "That was so romantic, I almost wanted to faint."

Sylvie sighed as well. "Nicholette should have pretended to faint in his arms, then he wouldn't have put her down so quickly."

I blushed at the thought of Mr. Hawthorne's arms around me. Had he also thought of that moment a thousand times since?

Mabel turned to peek into the hall, took a long moment to listen to the footsteps still ascending, and then stood. "This is the most perfect opportunity..."

Sylvie stood as well. "For what?"

Lastly, I stood, although I didn't know what Mabel was getting at.

She put a finger to her lips. "Just follow me."

So we did, and she guided us through the large pocket door at the far end of the room into a back parlor, and through that room and another set of pocket doors to the dining room. There were just as many finely appointed pieces of furniture in this back parlor and dining room as there had been in the front parlor, including an upright piano. But unlike the first two rooms, the entire left side of the dining room was made up of a dark wood-paneled buffet and many built-in drawers and various sizes of cabinet doors. The dining room furniture rivaled that of my parents', which was, again, so odd.

To my surprise, Mabel headed straight for one of the tall cabinet doors and opened it. There were a number of coats hanging there, and I wondered what on earth Mabel was up to. She certainly didn't need a coat in the middle of June.

But then she lifted the hem of her shirt and squatted into the bottom of the opening, where I heard her moving a piece of shelving. Sylvie was immediately beside her, as close as she could be in the tiny space, and before I realized what was going on, Mabel moved out of the way and Sylvie squeezed past her, squatting down through the little hidden passage Mabel had just opened.

With Sylvie already through, to who knew where, I had no choice but to follow, for so many reasons. And I was also uninterested in being left behind and perhaps having to tell Miss Abernathy about something I wasn't even certain I understood.

I crouched into the little space after Sylvie, which was just big enough for me to fit. I didn't know where we were headed, but I knew Sylvie was in front of me in the cramped darkness, for her giggles were continuous.

When I finally saw a dim light, I quickly realized it was from another cabinet door on the other side of the wall.

Sylvie had pushed open the door of this other cabinet and climbed out before me, then helped me stand and step out, and then Mabel behind me.

I realized, quite suddenly, that we'd just climbed out of an exact replica of the built-in cabinet and buffet we'd climbed into, only this room on the other side of the wall was set up with a dresser, a mirror standing in the corner, and a large, masculine four-poster canopy bed.

And if my guess was correct, I was standing in Mr. Cal Hawthorne's side of the double house. Which meant...

"Is this your brother's house? His bedchamber?" I asked.

"But of course. He doesn't use the upstairs, so he converted the dining room into his bedchamber," Mabel replied, already searching the counter of the buffet in the dim light from the curtained-off windows, as if she'd lost something terribly important.

"What are we doing here?" I asked, horrified at the thought of being found, especially in his dining room-turned-bedchamber. "We should go back."

"Oh, please stay. It will only take a minute, what I want to do, and...isn't it adventurous?"

"*Oui!*" Sylvie exclaimed from behind me. "And he'll never know."

"But if he were to find out—"

Mabel grabbed my hand and pressed her back to the closed door of the built-in cabinet. "Cal's never home during the day, no matter what day it is. You have nothing to worry about."

"What cause could you possibly have to sneak into his house? And why is there a passage like that through the cabinet in the first place?"

"I made it," was her shocking answer. She guided me, by force, to the other side of the room, toward her brother's bedside table, and began searching the titles of the books piled there.

"What did you say?"

"I finished digging it out last week, but I hadn't the nerve to sneak through yet."

"*C'est incroyable,*" Sylvie uttered with a whisper from across the room.

"What on earth did you dig through a wall with?"

"A hammer and a tool called a wrecking bar. Isn't that the most wonderful name for something that can tear a wall apart?"

For the first time since sneaking through her secret passage into her brother's side of the double house, I realized bits of chalky dust covered her dress. I looked down at my own and Sylvie's. Yes, all three of us were covered with little particles of the destroyed wall. "And where did you get these...tools?" I asked.

"They were in the barn. I didn't know what they were at first, only that I needed something, and I figured they would work for what I needed to do. Some boy caught me trying to take them into the house and asked me what I was doing, and he told me what they were and how to use them. But even with that bit of instruction, it took me ages to accomplish."

"And your mother doesn't know a thing about it? What about your maid?"

"They haven't a clue. Sally doesn't use the far cabinet much, only for our winter coats. And Mother is always abed in her room upstairs, toward the front of the house, and never heard a thing."

What an odd girl Mabel was. She was almost as fascinating as her brother, but in such a different way.

"You must swear to secrecy not to tell a soul. I think Cal's been hiding something from me for the last year or so. I can tell something's going on. I just haven't figured out what yet."

"Perhaps he has a very good reason for hiding whatever it is from you. Sometimes, it is best that we not know all the details about everything."

"I promise," Sylvie said.

"And what about you, Nicholette?" Mabel asked, disregarding the fact that I'd yet to allow her to use my Christian name.

"Fine. I promise," I muttered.

"I'm going to find his journal, or his calendar, or something." Mabel hurried across the room again and opened the glass-faced cabinets above the buffet counter, beginning her search. "It's the whole reason I dug that hole through the wall in the first place. He keeps his house locked up and won't give anyone a key. Not even Mother, or Sally, so she can clean. Not that he's here much, or that the kitchen is used at all…but still. He has his valet do everything for him."

"Your brother has a valet?" Sylvie asked.

"Oh…I forgot. I wasn't supposed to say anything about that."

I took a step closer to the built-in cabinet, thinking it would be best if we all just went back to Mabel's mother's house as quickly as possible. "Is it possible that his valet could be home right now—downstairs, or possibly upstairs?"

"No. Bowers has Saturdays off." Mabel flipped through a small leather-bound book. "Just let me do this little thing, and we'll head back soon, I promise."

I truly wished I'd had this conversation—about the tools, the valet, the secrets—with her *before* thoughtlessly crawling through for Sylvie's sake. It would have given me so much insight to what kind of shenanigans Mabel Hawthorne was apt to create, and I would never have followed Sylvie without question.

But then again, I was glad I had.

Taking a step back, I took a moment to look around the semi-darkened room. Neither Mr. Hawthorne nor his valet were home, after all. And truly, once I took a look around at *his* house, I couldn't help but take it all in.

It was the opposite floor plan of his mother's house next door, but decorated so differently, as if he'd actually cared to take the time to decorate the rooms in this new house he'd built for himself in a much different fashion than his mother had wanted hers. Everything was dark, wood paneling halfway up the walls, and pleasant beige willow leaf wallpaper from the paneling to the crown molding at the eleven-foot ceilings. His furnishings were also dark. His four-poster bed had a red canopy top. My gaze traveled down to the bed, to the messy, half-undone covers revealing vibrant white sheets.

Embarrassed, I darted my attention to the next room. The opened pocket doors revealed a library with a huge carved desk situated in the middle, the back of his chair tucked into a space created by a large curtain-less bay window. The four corners of the room were lined with tall, floor-to-ceiling bookcases.

It was far too tempting not to want to step in, to look at his books, his things. Not that I thought he was hiding anything substantial from his sister. She was likely imagining something far more adventurous than what he was about.

As Mabel and Sylvie continued to snoop around Mr. Hawthorne's bedchamber, I crept into the small library, being sure not to move the pocket doors any wider than they'd been.

I immediately noticed the front parlor through another set of half-opened pocket doors, and that it was just as exquisitely decorated. Wallpapered walls, lush carpet covering the floor where two brown leather tufted chairs were set at either side of the fireplace, and a light brown chaise set in front of the windows facing the street.

He certainly did have good taste, but the more I learned about Mr. Hawthorne and his mother and sister, the more I realized what a strange conundrum their life seemed. And why were they there in Boston anyway? I knew, from what Bram and Evangeline Everstone had disclosed on the subject of Violet's cousin, that the family was originally from somewhere west of Boston, but they'd been living here in this house in South Boston for a number of years. And it was so odd that they lived as they did. Did not Miss Abernathy think so as well?

Or perhaps she knew more concerning the Hawthorne family than she wanted to let on.

As I walked around the perimeter of the sun-filled library, my sense of caution lightened a little, and I was able to look at everything through a new scope. This was Mr. Hawthorne's world, and I had been given a chance to study it, and a little bit of him, without disclosure.

At the center of his desk, a large, leather-bound Bible was open. I leaned closer to get a better look and found that it was opened to the book of Psalms. I smiled. It was the same book of the Bible I'd been reading through lately, and I recalled reading the verses he'd underlined:

"When I consider your heavens, the work of your fingers, the moon and the stars, which you have set in place, what is mankind that you are mindful of them, human beings that you care for them?"

Was Mr. Hawthorne also consumed by the idea of God's grace for us? That God cared for insignificant humans such as us, who could ultimately do so little for the realm of the Kingdom of God?

Walking around the desk, I found, to my surprise, a huge orange cat curled up on the seat of the padded desk chair. I stroked his head, and his eyes opened. "Hello there, pretty kitty."

The cat immediately stood and stretched, and then climbed onto the desk, rubbing his nose, head, and body against any part of me he could reach.

What a sweet cat. I smiled at the fact that Mr. Hawthorne had such a pet. I'd had cats as a child, but I hadn't had any kind of pet for a long time.

Mabel parted the pocket doors a little more and strolled into the room. "Oh, Pumpkin."

The cat hissed as Mabel walked toward the desk.

"He doesn't like me. He'd hiss at me all day long if he had the opportunity."

"What on earth did you do to make him hate you?"

"I tickled him when he was a kitten. I thought all kittens liked belly tickles, but apparently Pumpkin is the exception, and he has hated me ever since."

Pumpkin meowed and leapt from the desk onto my shoulder, surprising me by how very heavy he was. As I wrapped my arms around Pumpkin, I heard a terrifying sound from the front of the house—the echo of a key turn in the lock at the front door.

"Oh, my goodness, he's home," I whispered, carrying the cat to Mr. Hawthorne's darkened bedchamber. "Where is Sylvie?"

Mabel followed, closing the pocket door behind us, except for the last quarter inch, where it stuck. "She's already gone back through. Snooping around for so long made her nervous."

Well, she wasn't the only one.

5

Secrets

"One of the deep secrets of life is that all that is really worth
the doing is what we do for others."
—Lewis Carroll, *The Letters of Lewis Carroll*

I wished I'd had the forethought to listen to my nerves upon realizing where Mabel had taken me. Now there I was, with Mr.
Hawthorne about to come through his front door, and wouldn't he
hear us if we tried to sneak back through now?

The front door closed, and we heard voices; Mr. Hawthorne's
contagious laugh and that of another man. At least, I thought
there were only two of them. I couldn't tell how many there were
or what they were saying. The door from the bedchamber to the
hall was, fortunately closed, and the noises from the front of the
house were muffled as their voices traveled to us from the open
doors of the library.

I dropped the cat onto the bed and headed to the cabinet we'd
climbed through, which Sylvie had left ajar. Mabel came up behind
me, reached around me, and forced it closed. "Please don't go. This
is perfection. I'll be able to listen in on their conversation, and

41

maybe find out what's going on. And you'd make too much noise getting back through. We'd be caught, for sure."

The men's footsteps on the wood floor sounded from the hall, and Mabel grabbed my hand, pulling me to the other side of the room and flinging me behind the tall canopy bed. "Hide here. He won't see us, if he even comes back here."

Goodness, I hoped he wouldn't! I wouldn't know how to face him ever again.

Mabel joined me on the floor in the shadowy corner, but I didn't feel we were nearly as hidden as I would've liked.

The wheels of the desk chair squeaked as they rolled across the floor in the next room.

"That's odd. Pumpkin is almost always sleeping on this chair," Mr. Hawthorne said from the library. But then he asked, "Do you want tea?"

"No, I don't want you to bother. I know Bowers isn't here today."

Mabel couldn't seem to resist getting closer to the pocket door to listen better, so she crawled nearer to the opening, as quietly as possible, taking long moments between her every move, the skirt of her pink afternoon dress dragging behind her.

After imagining the view she would gain by doing so, simply picturing Mr. Hawthorne in the next room wasn't enough for me either. I found myself tiptoeing across the carpeted floor to join Mabel as she listened at the pocket doors. With the lights still out in the bedchamber and the heavy curtains covering the windows, I had nothing to worry about concerning them seeing a shadow through the crack between the doors. Mabel crouched on the floor while I stood above her, squinting, trying my best to get a glimpse of Mr. Hawthorne again.

Through the crack, I could see that he sat at the corner edge of his desk, and watching him, taking my fill of his tall form put to such relief, and for as long as I liked through that tiny crack between the doors, had a most satisfying effect on me. And it was still odd to feel such things. Since when had I ever been attracted to or paid attention, so acutely, to one specific man?

Never. Never in my life.

Mr. Hawthorne's friend sat in one of the upholstered chairs facing him, but I couldn't tell much about him since he was farther across the room. "We're running out of fresh, willing bait. Everyone we've used would surely be recognized."

"We'll get him this time." Mr. Hawthorne rubbed both hands down his face, seeming a bit exasperated. "We have to."

"We can always hope, but I know what you mean. Daring young women willing to pose as hapless girls for the sake of such a case aren't easy to come by. But you have to admit, we've learned a lot from our failed attempts."

Their words didn't make sense to me. Who did they need to get? Failed attempts at what? And what did *fresh bait* mean?

"How much longer do you think we have until the next try?" Mr. Hawthorne asked. "A few weeks perhaps?"

"What has you in such a sure-fire hurry to be done with it now, after all this time?" the man in the chair asked.

Mr. Hawthorne didn't answer, but he looked to the ceiling and blew out a long breath through his nose.

"If I had my guess, which I suppose you're going to let me have since you're not talking, this would be about a woman."

"I have a lot going on that wasn't there before, from so many directions, it seems…my family, this case, and yes…."

"A woman," his friend supplied.

"Yes, a certain very fine young lady."

Mabel tapped her finger on the toe of my boot and whispered, "He means you."

I couldn't help but smile, thinking it had to be true. But what did everything else they were discussing mean?

"And you want things to be cleared up so you—"

"For a multitude of reasons, like I said." Mr. Hawthorne picked up a white marble, ball-shaped paperweight from the desk and tossed it from hand to hand. "Her father and I are, well, you could consider us friends...at least, now...again...."

Mr. Hawthorne knew *her* father?

No matter what Mabel believed, he couldn't have been speaking about me, and the disappointment I felt—deep in my chest—crushed everything I thought had happened between us at the bookshop. The flirting must have indeed meant nothing to him, which further proved that I had no idea what I was doing and absolutely no grasp on the matters of courting.

He wouldn't have known my father, and they certainly weren't friends. I would have known of that, surely.

"I don't think he'd be too keen on my pursuing her while also dealing with this case." Mr. Hawthorne continued to focus on the paperweight, staring at it intently.

Did he mean a case concerning the police? Why had he anything to do with the police?

"We've caught enough of Ezra's henchmen," Mr. Hawthorne added. "He's got to feel the pressure, as well as feel the need to come take care of things himself."

"I think there's a high probability we'll apprehend him soon, though I have a feeling my soon wouldn't be considered soon enough for you. Do you know for certain if this very fine young lady is interested in being pursued by the likes of Cal Hawthorne?"

"If her response to me so far is any indication, and considering the connections between our families, then yes, I do think it has a fair chance of working out. It's just this case...."

"Well, let's hope you don't get shot again in the next month and destroy your chances with her altogether."

Shot...again? What kind of life did Cal Hawthorne lead that he would have been shot? Or had the chance of being shot again?

Suddenly, all my thoughts and hopes I'd had regarding him seemed incredibly off, and I didn't know what to think. I didn't want to think, in fact. Not if it resulted in facing such anxieties and reliving such painful memories.

But without warning, images of blood-stained clothing, discarded suit jackets, wadded-up shirtsleeves, and the look on William's face after he'd been mistakenly shot in the back bombarded my mind, and I felt ill. All of the compounding memories, the ones I'd so prayerfully kept away for the last two years, convalesced into one: William lying dead on the dining table, my ruined wedding dress, and the absolute nothingness my life had become for so many months afterward.

Mr. Hawthorne put down the marble paperweight, reached inside his coat, and pulled out a pistol, laying it on the desk as he stood. "Not that I think she'd have anything against the cause, but it's true...she probably wouldn't approve of my being shot."

These last words pulled me from my memories, and instead of focusing on what was going on inside the room, I was only able to stare at the sliver of light shining through the crack between the doors.

Danger. Everything they had discussed emanated *danger*.

I felt sick. Contradicting emotions swirled through me—confusion, joy, anger, fear—and all together, they overwhelmed me. I hated the fact that I cared, that I wanted the same things he did... to pursue this evident connection between us. Only, how could I now?

From inside the room, I heard Mr. Hawthorne sit in his desk chair, causing the wheels to squeak across the floor again. At the noise, Pumpkin jumped from the bed and jogged over to me in the semi-darkness.

Meowing at the closed door, he hopped onto the dresser next to me, and then onto my shoulder. I reached up to him, brought him into my arms, and he began to purr.

Mabel looked up at me holding the cat and whispered, "Traitor."

Pumpkin hissed, reached past my arm to swat at Mabel.

Mabel and I had both taken our focus off the crack we'd been peeking through—off the men on the other side of the door—and too late I realized what a ruckus the cat had made, for as I turned away to keep Pumpkin from jumping at Mabel, the pocket doors opened and sunlight glared in on us from the library's large bay window.

"May! What are you—? Oh dear God, you brought—?"

I swiveled around in time to see Mr. Hawthorne help his sister up from where she was crouched on the floor.

"How did you get in here?" he asked, focused entirely on his sister.

"I can explain, Cal—it's all my fault," Mabel said as she came to her feet.

"How are you here?" he reiterated, as if it were the only thing he would allow himself to think upon for the moment.

"You'll never believe me, so I'd better just show you."

"I wouldn't doubt it." Mr. Hawthorne's frustration at finding us there was etched into every angry line of his face, his blue eyes almost covered by his lowered brows. He hadn't looked at me, at least not since I'd turned around to face the situation, keeping hold of his giant orange cat.

As I remained motionless, Mabel walked from the doorway to the far corner, where the cabinet door we'd come through was located. Once beside it, she opened the door just as her brother threw back the curtains from the nearest window, filling the room with sunlight. He continued to ignore me as he followed Mabel to the open cabinet door and looked inside.

He would likely never speak to me again after this.

"I tore apart the wall between the built-in cabinets," she explained, pointing to the hole she'd dug between the two houses, quite innocently. As if she knew he would forgive her.

Mr. Hawthorne combed his fingers through his hair. He didn't look to be in a very forgiving mood to me.

"You will go back through right now, May, and we will discuss this in more detail later."

For the first time since I'd turned around and found him in the doorway, Mr. Hawthorne acknowledged my presence. As he looked me in the eyes, I noticed a whole range of emotions flash behind his cool exterior: fear and embarrassment, but at the fore-front of them all, worry.

And of course all of those sentiments were raging through him. He knew. He knew I'd heard everything he'd confessed to his friend—everything about the case, about having been shot… everything about me.

"I'm sorry May brought you into all of this."

I remained standing near the footboard of his bed, still hold-ing Pumpkin, who now seemed quite content. I was glued to the floor, not knowing what to say or do.

Mr. Hawthorne's friend stood in the doorway of the library, silently inspecting the situation. He was a young gentleman, pos-sibly nearing thirty or so. He looked from Mr. Hawthorne to me, and then back again. Then he looked to where Mabel was standing in the light shining in through the window.

"Philip, you remember my sister." Mr. Hawthorne stretched a hand to where Mabel stood beside him. "As you know, she contin-uously proves too venturesome for her own good. May, you recall meeting Officer Philip Underwood last summer?"

"Yes, I recall," was all Mabel answered, somewhat downcast.

Officer Underwood gave Mabel a most genuine smile. "It's good to see you again, Miss Hawthorne."

"And this," Mr. Hawthorne took a few steps in my direction. He reached for his cat, who went to him willingly. He again looked me in the eyes, as if trying to read me. "Mrs. Everstone, this is my friend, Officer Philip Underwood. Philip, this is Mrs. Nicholette Everstone."

I blushed profusely. I still hadn't said a single word since we'd been discovered. But what was there for me to say? There was nothing.

"It's a great pleasure, Mrs. Everstone," Officer Underwood uttered politely.

"And now, May, you're going to take Mrs. Everstone back home now, the same way you came."

"But the plaster—"

He swiped at the white dust covering her sleeve. It came off easily. "I'm sure you'll be able to clean up just fine. The fact that you're missing from the tea scheduled with Mother leads me to believe that no one will likely detect a few dust particles."

"You knew about the tea?"

"Of course I did." Still holding his cat, Pumpkin's front paws happily spread over his shoulder, Mr. Hawthorne crossed the room to the cabinet door and held it open. "Now please leave."

He didn't have to ask me twice. I skittered across the room with one aim: to leave this uncomfortably awkward situation posthaste.

When Mabel and I climbed back through to her mother's dining room, Sylvie opened the cabinet door for us. "I hear Miss Abernathy coming down the stairs. You've returned just in time."

After the three of us were adequately dusted off, we met Miss Abernathy in the front hall as she came to the foot of the long staircase.

"I'm so disappointed our visit didn't work out as planned, but perhaps you can meet Mrs. Hawthorne more fully on a day when she's feeling better." She walked us toward the front doors, where we collected our things. "At least they had a chance to spend some time with you, Mabel. Did you all have an enjoyable time?"

None of us answered outright, besides little yeses or nods, which didn't surprise me. It had been a trying afternoon for all of us. I felt as if I'd been in another time and place for the majority of the last half hour, while I'd been snooping through Mr. Cal Hawthorne's house.

How could I have done such a thing? Everything about the afternoon left me horrified at myself and disappointed in a million different ways besides.

On the drive home, I stared, unseeing, out the carriage window at the blur of buildings and trees, but I saw so much beyond that. Memories from my wedding jolted through my mind. William kissing me the morning of our wedding day, my gleaming white wedding dress covered in his blood.

Forcing my mind from the recollections, I instead thought back to Mr. Hawthorne's angry disappointment at finding us in his house. Who was he, really? Was he an undercover police officer? A detective? And what did it mean that his sister didn't even know?

6

New Directions

"A word in earnest is as good as a speech."
—Charles Dickens, *Bleak House*

We all know Nicholette is going to outshine everyone else at every event she attends this summer, Guinevere, darling. Now that her cards have been sent out indicating her reentrance to society, the men are simply going to flock to her, as they always have."

At the mention of my attending social events to my mother, I stopped outside the front parlor of the Everstones' impressive mansion and waited to hear more. Knowing Miss Claudine Abernathy, she would have plenty to say, beyond what I'd just heard from her.

"She's still so young," our hostess, Mrs. Evangeline Everstone, added. "You are going to allow her to fraternize, are you not?"

I was honestly surprised she cared one way or another. I'd only just met her in the last two months and knew her to be a woman of few words.

After no verbal answer for some time, Mrs. Annabelle Summercourt—another of my mother's friends—continued,

"Marrying again is the best thing she could do now, if you want her to successfully move on from this unfortunate turn of events."

"You must encourage her to marry again, quickly," Miss Abernathy reiterated with finality.

Though I didn't especially like the topic of their conversation, I lingered in the hall, waiting for more.

"We only just arrived home," my mother said. "Do you truly think she won't be judged too harshly by society if she marries again so soon? That there has been sufficient time for her to heal from such an ordeal?"

For months, I'd been thinking about what my life would be like once I was out of mourning, and now that I'd been out for almost a month, the concept still seemed quite foreign. How would this transition go? My mother had seemed much more reluctant about my next steps than my father, as her words now confirmed.

"Certainly there has. It's been over two years."

It took me a moment to place the male voice behind this callous addition to the conversation, but then I recalled it had to be Alexander Summercourt, who had just moved back to Boston from New York City. He must have arrived at Everwood with his mother while I'd been out of the room.

"I, for one, think she should be quite over what happened," he continued.

"Alex," his mother reprimanded. "You cannot say such things, not having ever been in a similar situation yourself. And although her mourning is over and we will encourage her to marry, she may not be as ready as you would like her to be."

"We will see," was his only reply.

Oh goodness. Apparently, Alex thought I was quite the catch now that I had William's inheritance as well as my own.

"Don't forget, everyone remembers exactly when William died," Mother responded. "The horrid details were written up in newspapers all over the country. Don't think they'll not be watching her every move. And what if it ends up that a number of the gentlemen, who will no doubt vie for her attention, are only after her money?" she asked, with good reason. "She's settled for life now that Bram Everstone has bequeathed William's fifth of the inheritance to her."

"Dear, the same could have been said for her marrying William," Miss Abernathy refuted. "He could have doubted her love because of how the whole thing was arranged between the families, but he didn't. Anyone could tell he adored her, and that was all that mattered to him. We have to trust she'll be able to discern such things for herself, as we have all had to learn to do throughout the years."

"I don't know....I know Nicholas thinks she should be ready..." was Mother's quiet response.

"I'm certain she is, and I know just where she should live."

"Live?" Mother asked.

"She'll need a house when she's married, and Hilldreth Manor will soon be on the market."

"What are you saying, Claudine?" Mrs. Summercourt exclaimed. "Hilldreth cannot be *sold*—where would you live?"

"I'm going to move to Everston to be near Estella and her new family. Letty Hawthorne put the idea in my mind last summer with all her wishful plans, and although I know she will never actually move away from her children, I do not have the same problem."

"But you have us," I heard Mother say quietly.

"It is but a day's train ride away. We will still see one another."

"So you're planning to move away?" Mother continued.

"And who better to move into Hilldreth Manor than Nicholette? She'll need somewhere to live once she's married and settled again, and I know just who I'd like to see her end up with," Miss Abernathy said.

"And who is that?" Mrs. Summercourt asked, sounding annoyed, for it obviously wasn't her son, who was present, that Miss Abernathy had in mind.

Miss Abernathy giggled. "Violet's cousin, Cal Hawthorne."

I gripped the curtain and leaned closer to the opening of the parlor to better listen.

"He's young, handsome, and available," she continued. "Nicholette hasn't seen him yet, but just you wait until she does. They'll make a spectacularly smashing couple."

Of course, she said this not realizing that I'd indeed met the man—whom she'd described quite accurately—two times by then. Two times burned into my memory that wouldn't let me rest at night.

I blushed profusely at the annoyingly delightful thought, the thought of being married…to *him*. The blush, at suddenly thinking far too much of "handsome and available" Cal Hawthorne, traveled down my neck and back, heating me most uncomfortably. But then I shook the image away…what was I thinking?

"Yes, Nicholas has mentioned him. Seems he's known him quite well in past years, I suppose from something to do with the bank," Mother added. "And Bram has been specifically interested in introducing him to Nicholette, hasn't he, Evie?"

"*Oui*," Mrs. Evangeline Everstone said. "He is a fine young gentleman, quite sought after now that Violet marrying Vance has brought him out of obscurity. They're from a fine family, but living in a double townhouse in South Boston hardly seems right."

"Oh posh." Miss Abernathy scolded her friend. "They like the quiet life, is all. And Nicholette has seen where he lives. I took her to see his mother and sister for tea, remember? Where they live isn't terrible; it's just much smaller."

"You don't think they're related to that scandalous Hawthorne family of Westborough, do you, Claudine?" Mrs. Summercourt asked. "Everyone from Westborough to Boston has heard of the stigma behind the name Chauncey Hawthorne."

The name jogged a distant memory, and I vaguely recalled once meeting someone by that name years and years past...but there had been nothing scandalous about the gentleman or his family back then. Honestly, I couldn't remember a single thing about him other than his peculiar name and that we must have socialized in similar circles.

"Whatever happened?" my mother asked, apparently lacking information, having been in Europe for the last two years with Father and me.

"It is widely and infamously known," Mrs. Summercourt answered, "that Mr. Chauncey Hawthorne II, upon his death, left the lion's share of his fortune to his mistress and their six very young children rather than his wife and his legitimate children."

"It's an abomination that such things can even be done," Miss Abernathy practically exclaimed. "They certainly cannot be undone!" After what seemed a long pause of consideration, she went on. "Afterwards, the rumors flew, for he'd been known as an exceptional man of Christian character, and now the disgrace of what the scoundrel had done to his family as his last rightful act on earth has proven to be too much a burden to bear. The family, his wife and his legitimate children, haven't been seen or heard from for years."

"I would never show my face again either," Mother added.

"But didn't I hear that a great uncle left everything he had to them, giving them his vast fortune in restitution for what his nephew had done to his family?" Mrs. Everstone asked.

"Still, even with that recent news, the whole thing is disgraceful. And still no one knows where they are. It all sounds very shady to me."

It hardly seemed fair to me to blame the family left behind after such an awful occurrence, no matter who they were or where they were living now.

"And I'm quite certain our friends are not related to *those* Hawthornes," Miss Abernathy continued. "Can you imagine? Cal and Mabel—and Violet, I might add—related to this Chauncey Hawthorne fellow? What a preposterous thought." She laughed. "I think Violet would know that much about her own family."

"I wouldn't be so certain about Violet knowing anything," Mrs. Summercourt said. "The families had been estranged for decades, until Violet moved down to Boston from Maine last year."

"Are you not good friends with their mother, Claudine?" Mother asked. "Have you not asked about their connection to Chauncey Hawthorne?"

"Oh, believe me, I've done my best," Miss Abernathy answered. "She doesn't come right out and say much—she isn't feeling well these days, you know—but Letty's explained to me enough that I believe they're far enough removed from the Chauncey Hawthorne family that it likely has no influence on the reasons they are living in South Boston. She'd told me that her late husband—and to be clear, his name was *Robert*, not *Chauncey*—and Violet's father, Edward, grew up in Westborough. Edward met and married Violet's mother in Maine and stayed in that area and was therefore estranged from the rest of the family. They never saw him again; they only wrote a few nondescript letters back and forth over the years."

"They *are* wonderful people," I barely heard Mrs. Summercourt add.

I had to agree. Miss Abernathy's last comments about Mr. Hawthorne's family seemed to create a balm for my soul, after thinking that Mr. Hawthorne and his sister could possibly be linked to such a family—a family which Miss Abernathy regarded as so entirely scandalized.

Not that I knew why it mattered.

"Well then, it's settled," Miss Abernathy stated. "Hopefully we will see Nicholette married again by the end of the year."

Suddenly I didn't want their conversation to go on, so I hurried from my hiding spot into the parlor through the thick, lavender curtains half covering the room's entrance.

At the sight of me, Alex stood and bowed in greeting. "Nicky. We were just talking about how half of Back Bay is still in love with you," he said with an overly friendly wink, "despite your lengthy absence and what I've heard of your repugnant wardrobe of late."

"Thank you, Alex," I said, trying to keep things as they always had been between us—with absolutely no encouragement on my part. He hadn't been there when I'd left the room, and I hadn't seen him in over two years.

"You are a vision of loveliness, Nicholette, no matter what you're wearing. It makes my heart happy to see you in your colors again." Miss Abernathy stood, and I noticed how slowly she crossed the room with the help of her cane. Perhaps some days she simply needed it more than others, but I wasn't so sure. When she reached me, she took my hands in hers. "We are all tremendously happy you have returned to society. We were just discussing how you have been sorely missed."

"Have you?" I asked, knowing very well that the discussion had been so much more than that.

"And that you're still so lovely, dearest. As attractive as ever, and quite possibly ready for a new husband." There was just the tiniest little glint in Mrs. Summercourt's eye as her gaze skittered past her son. She obviously wanted me to marry her middle son.

Of course she did. I was one of the wealthiest, youngest widows in all of New England now.

"But…." I looked to my mother, who had now stood as well. Yes, I had heard their conversation, but it hadn't convinced me that it would be brought up to me directly for many weeks, or perhaps months. "But my mourning for William..." I stated dumbly, unprepared to actually have the conversation. "I've only just...."

"I'm sure everyone knows you still miss William," Miss Abernathy crooned, "but perhaps it is best you find someone new to marry. Anyone who knows the situation would surely understand."

The pursuit of another husband.

And knowing just who she meant to push me toward had my stomach turning in knots.

She didn't know. None of them would be happy to link Mr. Hawthorne and me together if they knew of his involvement with the police. Would they?

"Nicholette, dear, we know you loved William," Mother added. "No one can blame you for the way things turned out—"

"And I for one cannot wait to see you enchant the multitudes again." This startling admission came from the entryway to the main hall—from William's practically look-alike brother, Vance Everstone.

The man who *was* to blame.

It had been since my wedding that I'd last seen him. And for all my claims of being over William's death, I could not profess to be over his murder. Or why it had happened.

"Now, now, Nicky, try not to look so harsh," he said as he stood in the massive twenty-foot doorway, his hands at his hips, most disapprovingly.

I'd not realized my vexed thoughts had been so displayed upon my face, but they must have been, for the young woman standing next to Vance—presumably, his newly wedded wife, Violet—looked at me as if she were scared to move forward. As Vance stepped farther into the room, she kept him back with a tight grip upon his left elbow.

Vance motioned his wife forward, and I got an even better look at her. This adorably shy creature with short blonde hair wasn't what I had expected as the kind of woman able to bend him into the devoted husband I'd heard he'd been transformed into. And how on earth had the Vance Everstone I'd known come to attract such an amiable, unassuming girl? How had he made such a girl fall in love with him? I was quite stunned, but not enough to remain silent.

I stepped toward the entrance to the hall. "Vance, please introduce me to your wife." I extended my hand.

Violet reached out, took my hand, and immediately relaxed.

After the introduction was complete, Vance smiled down at his wife, a gesture I didn't recognize, for he hadn't been one to do much of that before. What a difference she had made. But perhaps it was more than just Violet's influence.

Alex stepped up behind me, as did both of our mothers. "Vance, it's been a long time—I think your father's wedding last summer." He shook Vance's hand. "And it's nice to see you again, Mrs. Everstone. It seems as if our old rakish Vance has turned a new leaf, indeed, and is treating you well."

Vance smirked. "Of course I am."

Violet's cheeks turned a sweet shade of pink, but the look she gave Vance from behind his back was pure adoration. I was again completely stunned, and I felt a deep stab of regret mixed with jealousy for how entirely Violet obviously adored her husband... and he, one so undeserving. It had been Vance's previously reckless way of living that had brought the tragedy about in the first place.

Violet must have seen something of my inner pain, for she gently butted her shoulder between Vance and I and went on to make more conversation. Which made me wonder...could anyone else tell just how much I'd grown to dislike Vance—even more than I had before—since William's death?

I hadn't seen him, of course, since he and Violet had returned from Maine. But he had often been a part of our conversations in the last year. From what I recalled, I'd always tried my best not to say anything regarding Vance and Violet living in my Fairstone, when the subject had come up.

I would have to go into the house again someday, but I hoped it wouldn't be anytime soon. It was already difficult enough to know everyone watched me, studied me from the other side of the gossip pages, waiting for me to do something interesting. Like attend a wedding.

I didn't even know how I'd make it through Clyde Summercourt's wedding, which I knew was coming up, after the way mine to William had ended.

And my marrying Cal Hawthorne was certainly out of the question, no matter that Miss Abernathy thought we'd make a "spectacularly smashing couple." And especially no matter that I'd entertained silly, high hopes about him after our unconventional introduction at the bookshop. But that had been before I'd learned what he was about. He was much too daring for my tastes.

No, Miss Abernathy was wrong. She didn't know. She hadn't heard him speak to the undercover police officer he spent much of his time shadowing. She hadn't heard them joke about how he'd been shot and he could very well be shot again.

If she'd known all of that, and then thought back to my wedding day, I was certain she'd change her mind. We would not suit, no matter how well we got on upon first meeting.

7

Rochester Farms

"When the character of a man is not clear to you,
look at his friends."
—Japanese proverb

About two weeks later, Father decided he wanted to take me to pick out a new horse. My last had died shortly before my wedding to William and replacing Shiloh had been the last thing on my mind at that time, and since, considering we'd been traveling through Europe for so long.

We traveled south of Boston by train to a town called Quincy without much to say. I knew this was a breeder we'd never bought from before, and that he'd come to make a name for himself internationally when it came to Morgan horses, but I truly didn't know much about picking out a horse. It was the first time Father had ever wanted to include me with such a decision. He'd simply presented to me both of the horses I'd had the honor of owning, and I'd loved both of them.

When we arrived to Rochester Farms, a sprawling farm of open pastures, country woods, and massive flower and vegetable gardens greeted us as we traveled down a long, tree-lined drive that led straight to a massive, Victorian-style brick mansion.

We came to an office where we met Mr. Rochester, the owner of the horse farm, and told him what we were in market for. After speaking with him for a few minutes, we were given leave to look around the stables, and I headed out to the yard before my father, too excited to wait.

Father finally left the office and rejoined me in the yard.

"I don't know how I'll ever decide from looking at so many. I'm used to you just giving me a horse and loving it." I studied the pamphlet, scanning the many Morgan horses listed. But then my attention snagged on the horse at the end of the list. "I'd like to take a look at this British horse listed. It says he's a Gypsy Vanner—whatever that means—and his name is Fergus."

"You can pick out whichever horse you like best." Father grinned. "I was trying to narrow it down to the ones most like Spark so they would match. But if you want something else, go ahead and pick it out."

When we finally reached the Gypsy Vanner's stall at the far end of the barn, we found he was a stout horse of a deep brown color, a white stripe down his nose, and four white, feathery "socks" on his feet. He was so different than a Morgan horse.

"Fergus." I stuck my hand through the bars of the wooden gate, and to my surprise, he stepped over to me and nudged his nose on my hand. His sweet brown eyes settled upon me.

He was the most gorgeous color brown I'd ever remembered seeing on a horse. He was perfection. "I know he doesn't match Spark. And Spark is beautiful, Father, with his champion blood-lines and all. But I think I'd rather have a horse like Fergus. He seems just like me." A little misplaced for the time being.

"All right, you'll have him."

"Oh, Fergus, you will be mine," I whispered through the gate.

Because Father ended up being the only person remotely interested in the Gypsy Vanner, he was able to get Fergus for nearly
nothing compared to what the champion Morgan horses were
going for. When we'd finished filling out the paperwork for the
purchase at the office, Mr. Rochester came up to Father, stopping
us as we were about to leave.

"Mr. Fairbanks, I found the young gentleman you were asking
to see."

"Yes, thank you for doing that for me, Rochester."

When Mr. Rochester departed, to my surprise, Mr. Cal
Hawthorne walked out from behind him, looking right at me with
a cunning smirk gracing his beautiful full lips.

He was the last person on earth I'd expected to see just then,
and I quickly realized my guard was not nearly where it needed to
be for such a situation. I tried desperately to seem unaffected by
the sudden sight of him. But I wasn't though—not by half. Just
the thought of his name over the weeks since I'd seen him had created all kinds of awful, unsure feelings in me. My memories from
those two times I'd met him in the last month, would not, could
not, be reconciled. And then...if Mr. Hawthorne indeed knew
my father, he could very well have been speaking of me to Officer
Underwood when I'd been eavesdropping on their conversation.
The mere thought of that entire discussion sent a wave of anxious-
ness through me.

What was I supposed to say to him now?

"Nicholette, allow me to introduce a friend of mine, Mr. Cal
Hawthorne. He currently works here for Mr. Rochester in the
accounting department." Father took a step forward, forcing Mr.
Hawthorne to follow. "Cal, this is my daughter, of course, Mrs.
Nicholette Everstone."

Still genuinely shocked, I stood there, my chin slightly
dropped. So it was true. My father did know Mr. Hawthorne.
And he wanted to introduce him to me? And was that why we

had come to this new horse breeder, where Mr. Hawthorne just happened to work?

"It is good to meet you, Mrs. Everstone." Mr. Hawthorne remained smiling, directly at me, as if meeting me for the first time.

I extended my hand, and he enveloped my small fingers in his large ones, keeping eye contact. I couldn't deny that his figure was impressive; I knew from too much experience. And having him beside me again—after the last time in his bedchamber—was rather intimidating. Did that mean Mr. Hawthorne had indeed been speaking about me with Officer Underwood that day?

Mr. Hawthorne stood relatively close as our hands were clasped between us. I made a point not to look away, ignoring the butterflies in my stomach.

"Thank you, Mr. Hawthorne. It is, isn't it?" There was such a magnetic pull between us, I couldn't help but stay where I was, wanting more, waiting for more. Despite everything I knew, despite all of my unanswered questions.

His gaze remained on me for a few moments longer, and then he let go of my hand to shake my father's. "It's good to see you again, sir. You must be in the market for a horse?"

"As a matter of fact, we are," Father replied. "Since I'd heard from Vance Everstone that you worked for Rochester here, we thought we'd come to take a look, and also see if you were around."

"Did you end up finding what you were looking for today?"

"The only non-champion horse on the farm, I believe." Father glanced my way with a quizzical slant to his brow. Was he trying a gauge my response to Mr. Hawthorne? Or was he still puzzled about the horse I chose? "But yes, just what we were looking for, it seems."

"The Gypsy Vanner? He was a bit of a random addition to the group. No papers or bloodlines, but a good solid little gelding."

"I think he's perfect," I said, in an effort to join the conversation.

"I've never seen a horse like him," Father said.

"Nor have I, and I've seen my fair share working for Rochester."

"I suppose we'll see you at the Summercourt wedding coming up in August?" Father asked.

"My family has been invited."

"I don't think I'll be attending the wedding," I blurted.

Or any wedding ever again, to be at all honest. Not after the horrendous affair mine had turned out to be.

"Are the Summercourts not old family friends of yours?" Mr. Hawthorne asked me.

"Yes," Father supplied. "And of course Nicholette will be there."

My stomach turned to knots.

"I should be there," Mr. Hawthorne said. "I'm hoping, by then, to be finished with a complicated project that's been taking a considerable amount of my time of late. We're hoping it will only be another few weeks." The look on his face was indecipherable, as if he were unsure about something, or concerned.

It was about the case, of course.

Mr. Hawthorne gave a half shrug. "Beyond seeing you at the wedding, I likely won't have much time for socializing."

"Then I suppose we'll have to be content waiting to see you at the wedding, won't we, Nicky?" Father asked pointedly, obviously trying to get me to make a promise to attend the dreaded affair in Mr. Hawthorne's presence.

"Yes, we will have to wait and see," was all I allowed.

I spied the receipt of payment for Fergus in Father's hand and remembered that my new horse would be waiting for us outside. And really, I was ready for this surprise visit with Mr. Cal Hawthorne to be over. "We should probably go. The horse is likely—"

"Ah, yes, they've been tying Fergus to the back of our carriage, and I'll want to inspect. It was good seeing you again, Mr. Hawthorne. I do hope you won't mind an invitation for you, your mother, and sister to dine at Faircourt sometime soon," Father offered, shocking me with this sudden bout of hospitality.

"That's a gracious offer," Mr. Hawthorne answered with a smile, "and one I'm sure we won't be able to refuse, Mr. Fairbanks, once I have more time in my schedule. And yes, don't let me hold you up."

Then he turned to me. "Well, I wish you much love with your Gypsy Vanner, Mrs. Everstone. It makes me glad to know he'll be yours and treasured for the special horse that he is."

"Thank you. And he will—I will, I promise," I uttered awkwardly, knocked completely off kilter by his responses to me.

With nothing more to say, Father and I walked toward the carriage.

As we were leaving with Fergus tied to the back, I looked upon the hilly fields of Rochester Farms. I didn't especially feel like talking. I had too much going on inside. But after thinking and rethinking the exchange I'd had with Mr. Hawthorne, I needed more answers, and perhaps Father could be just the one to help.

But before I could say a word, Father asked, "Nicholette, may I ask what you thought of meeting Mr. Hawthorne today?"

"He's very…um, he's very…."

"Yes, well, I saw your face while we were speaking with him, and I can imagine what you thought on that count."

"Father!"

"He is a good looking boy, you have to admit."

Though *boy* wasn't quite the word I would have chosen. He was much too attractive, and had already been much, *too much*… on my mind of late. *That's* what I thought of him.

After a long while of staring out the window, I asked, "Father, you do realize that your friend, Mr. Hawthorne, is Violet's cousin, don't you?"

"Of course."

"Why have you never brought him up before if you've known him so entirely well?"

"I don't speak to you and your mother about work. I never have. The subject wouldn't have come up."

"Does that have anything to do with it?"

"He worked for me once, a few years ago."

"Are we speaking about the same Mr. Hawthorne? Mr. Cal Hawthorne?"

"Yes, dear." He seemed mildly entertained by my confusion. "And it would please me immensely to have him acquainted with my daughter."

Did Father seriously want me to become interested in Mr. Hawthorne?

Well, I didn't need any help in that regard. I was already too interested, in too many ways, despite knowing better.

"He doesn't seem...safe," I answered quietly.

"I'm surprised at you, Nicky, thinking up wild antidotes regarding people you hardly know."

Did I not know Mr. Cal Hawthorne? I felt as if I did—I felt as if I'd known him for the longest time...and that getting to know him better would prove to be an absolutely fascinating adventure.

Which was the last thing I needed.

"And why ever would you say such a thing?" Father continued.

"Just an impression I got...." But then I took my chance to ask, "Do you know what his family is like?"

"Wealthy, well-respected, for the most part. His grandfather helped bring the railroads through Westborough and left quite an inheritance for his descendants."

"Did you happen to know him while he was married?"

"You know he is a widower then, do you?"

"I've heard mention of it before... from Miss Abernathy."

"Somehow that doesn't surprise me," he stated.

"Now, Father, before you—"

"Were you also told that it was the same sort of arrangement your mother made with Grace Everstone when you were younger? Only his wife had been ill, and it was obvious to everyone that she would likely die young. But no one imagined she would pass away a mere three months after their wedding."

Although I'd known he was widowed from our first meeting, and I'd heard a little about it from Miss Abernathy, hearing this information now, from my father, stirred a peculiar ache in my chest. Something like jealousy, which was ridiculous. I tried to convince myself that it had to do with wishing I'd had three months married to William, but I knew that wasn't it. Being married for one day and widowed had been difficult enough. I couldn't even imagine if we'd been married for three months before he'd been murdered.

But that really wasn't it at all. I was jealous that someone else had had the fortune to be married to Mr. Cal Hawthorne.

Even as I told myself over and over and over that I didn't want him.

"He'd worked for me for only a short time before the wedding, and then for maybe a year after. And it probably had a lot to do with why I'd grown so attached to him. He lived here in Boston alone, his family all still in Westborough at the time. His wife had been from New York, if I remember right, so her family wasn't around either. It was such a trying time for the boy, I couldn't help but take him under my wing."

I knew Father had always wished for more children besides myself. It wasn't a secret to anyone that he would have especially loved having a few sons, as all of his closest friends had. They'd all seemed to have more than enough. And then he'd been blessed with only me.

"I've been worried about him for a long time now, for I hadn't known what had come of him over the last few years. You see, when he stopped working for me at the bank, he just left one day without a word and never came back. Which wasn't like him at all."

I had to agree. I couldn't imagine the Mr. Hawthorne I'd experienced those three times I'd met him in recent weeks doing such a thing, and it made me wonder.

And I didn't want to wonder. I wanted to stop thinking about him altogether.

But I couldn't seem to make that happen.

That he had somehow made such an impression on Father all those years ago, and the fact that they had formed such a lasting friendship that could be picked back up so easily said much for Mr. Hawthorne's character.

"Where did he go?" I asked.

"I was unable to find out a thing about him for the whole following year, no matter how I searched. And then your mother decided we'd take the extended vacation to Europe for you... I thought the idea of ever seeing him again was hopeless."

"You never found out why he'd left the bank without a word? And was that three years ago, then?"

"It was. Just about the same time you'd become engaged to William. And I did find out the reason. And everything considering, I decided to forgive him," Father contributed. "I hope you don't mind that I brought you here today to meet him. We did need to buy you a horse, after all."

"What was the reason he gave up his job working for you at Massachusetts Bank to work for some horse breeder?"

"The boy had his reasons, Nicky, and sometimes it is not for us to know everything. You know that. And right now, that's something that doesn't need to concern you."

This felt like a slap in the face. Since when would Father intentionally want to keep information—which I desperately wanted—away from me?

Father looked at me suspiciously. "It pleases me that you want to know Cal better, Nicky, it truly it does. But you'll have to get your answers from him as you get to know him better yourself, if you want them that badly."

After traveling the rest of the way to the train station in silence and then having Fergus loaded onto the cargo car of the train into Boston, we made it to our compartment. A few minutes after the train started on its way, and after a long silence between us, Father spoke up. "We received an invitation in the post this morning for a dinner party at Everthorne in August."

"Which I'll also not be attending."

"You will go, Nicholette." Father huffed. "We've already been too lax in our social responsibilities since returning to Boston. It is time we stepped out more."

But why did our first outings have to be a wedding and then a dinner at Everthorne?

I simply wasn't ready to go into the mansion that used to be mine for such a short period of time. Even knowing that Vance and Violet had renovated the interior, I still didn't think I would be able to stand a visit yet. Then, of course, there was the fact that it was Vance's dinner party. And I hated Vance.

He now had everything I'd ever wanted. Everything I'd had for a split moment.

And it was his fault it was gone.

"Cal's sister, Mabel Hawthorne, will be there." Father's voice roused me from my haunted memories. "I thought you'd be looking forward to seeing her again."

"Oh...yes," I allowed.

Mabel and Sylvie and I did get together on a regular basis, usually at Everwood, where Sylvie lived with her mother and stepfather. And Mabel had never once brought up what we'd done that day, for which I was deeply thankful. I didn't like to think back on it myself, for I'd never done anything so embarrassing in all my life.

"Cal will likely be there, too, of course, in case getting to know him better is indeed of interest to you."

"Father."

"He's become quite the eligible bachelor now that Violet has married Vance, you know. And I heard Evangeline and Claudine discussing him the other day in great detail. It seems they're hoping he'll snag your attention."

"Is that right?" I finally uttered. "They don't seem to be the only ones." I slid a knowing glance across the cabin, directed straight at Father's brownish-hazel eyes that matched my own. And he grinned, realizing he'd been caught.

I didn't like this at all. The knowledge that Father desired for me to become so closely acquainted with Mr. Cal Hawthorne spoke volumes.

And it didn't make any sense. Not now that I'd seen in what a bizarre manner he and his mother and sister lived their lives. Not that it was a bad way of living, just so strange.

Then, of course, there was the whole part of his life that none of them knew about.

"Dearest, I know it might be difficult to see Everthorne, but do try to think more about your future than your past. You have so many years ahead of you."

Fighting back tears, I couldn't answer.

Father reached into the space between us on the bench seat and grabbed my hand, squeezing it for a brief moment. Then he let go. "I'm sorry you've had to go through this. I do hope keeping you away from Boston for the last two years was the best thing. You don't know how we've worried about this transition you've had to make back into society. I don't want you to feel pressured to marry, but I want you to know, it would make me happy if you did."

"Really?" I asked, genuinely shocked. "Why?"

"You know we weren't able to have any more children after we had you…and I've missed that. Being a parent is a wondrous thing, daughter, and I think I'd enjoy being a grandfather."

Ah, so that was his reasoning. Knowing this changed so much about my perception of how things had been in the last few years. Perhaps he and Mother hadn't been so worried about my reentrance to society as they were anxious about how things would go for me after I did so.

"I'm looking forward to that too someday, Father."

And it was the truth. I did want to marry again, to rebuild my life, to become a mother someday.

"When is the dinner party?" I asked, knowing full well I was giving Father too much hope that I'd eventually agree.

"The eleventh of August. And I see that look on your face, Nicky." Father grinned knowingly. "You look like you're considering."

"I'll think about it, Father. But I'm not making any promises."

8

Riverway Park

"Willing is not enough; we must do."
—Johann Wolfgang von Goethe

A week later, while I'd been traveling through town with my parents, calling on many of their old friends to request items for the silent auction at the upcoming Charity Ball, we happened to stop at our favorite restaurant for lunch. As my parents and I made our way into the front door of the restaurant, however, I immediately noticed Vance and Violet Everstone sitting at a table in the corner, along with Sylvie Boutilier and Mr. Cal Hawthorne.

Jealousy swarmed through me at seeing Mr. Hawthorne seated next to Sylvie, and I tried to tamp it down, to make it disappear forever, but there seemed nothing I could do. I hated that I still had such severe reactions at just the thought of him, and especially the sight of him. Despite how I fought the feelings he induced, it was a constant, losing battle.

But why were Mr. Hawthorne and Sylvie there with Vance and Violet? Were they trying to make a match between them the same way Miss Abernathy wanted to match him with me?

Ugh, what a thought. How would I ever stand to be friends with her again?

They didn't notice us come into the restaurant at first, but Father fixed that when he led Mother and me over to their table as we were being shown to our own table across the room.

Fortunately, we only stayed long enough to say hello and then moved on to our table for our meal. But my relaxed meal with my parents had become anything but that knowing that Mr. Hawthorne sat next to the French, charming Sylvie Boutilier on the other side of the room.

Sylvie, who didn't have the guilt of being found snooping in his house hanging over her head. Yes, she'd been with us for a moment, but Mr. Hawthorne wouldn't have known that. He'd only known his sister and I had been there.

When we finished our lunch, our friends had long since left the restaurant, and I was forced to imagine Mr. Hawthorne spending the rest of his afternoon with Sylvie, which had me in a particular mood. I certainly didn't like it. Why was it that the sight of this one man—no matter the situation—did more things to my heart than any other man before him? Why did *he* have such influence on my emotions, when I didn't even want to like him?

When we came out of the restaurant to call for our carriage, we realized that our friends hadn't left after all. Both Vance and Mr. Hawthorne stood next to Vance's large carriage, which was parked next to the sidewalk a little ways down the street, and we made our way over.

"Glad to see you are still here," Father said, patting both Vance and Mr. Hawthorne on the back. As we walked up to the carriage, Mother and I noticed Violet and Sylvie inside, keeping out of the sun, and waved to them.

"We were wondering if you wanted to join us for our excursion to Riverway Park," Vance said. "It's a shame not to enjoy the beautiful weather we're having."

"It is a wonderful day, but unfortunately we are taking advantage of it in our own way, calling upon our friends who have volunteered to donate items for the Charity Ball's silent auction."

"That reminds me," Vance said. "I have something I'd like to include as well. We weren't in town when you initially went about asking for donations."

"Very well, we'll always find room for something more. I have a feeling the auction items this year are going to make for a successful benefit."

Vance looked at Mr. Hawthorne for a moment, which caught my attention, for I hadn't looked at either Vance or Mr. Hawthorne until then. Since walking up to them, I had kept back with Mother as Father had his conversation.

But then Violet asked, "Could you, at least, spare Nicholette?"

My eyes darted to Violet, and then Mr. Hawthorne, who looked as surprised as I felt at the request.

"Well, I don't see why not," Father said. "What do you think, Nicholette? Would you rather go with your friends to the Riverway than continue on with us?"

I was torn. I did, and I didn't. I wanted to see more of Mr. Hawthorne, yet I knew it was a terrible idea to do so. Then there was Sylvie. It could end up that Vance and Violet walked together through the park and Mr. Hawthorne and Sylvie were to walk together. Would I merely find myself bringing up the end of the line all on my own? That didn't sound like a good time. But then there was also the alternate possibility—that I would be the one walking alongside him....

Which *was* a terrible idea.

It really was.

However, I found I couldn't say anything but, "I—I suppose."

Father took my arm and guided me closer to the carriage, next to Mr. Hawthorne.

"That is perfect. We were just taking Sylvie to pay a call on a dear friend of hers from finishing school for the afternoon, and we have a few hours until it is time to take her home."

It wasn't perfect. It was terrible. And I was foolish.

Once we said goodbye to my parents, Vance entered his carriage, leaving Mr. Hawthorne to help me in to sit between Violet and Sylvie on the forward-facing bench. He then climbed in, and we were off.

As I sat there, facing Mr. Hawthorne in the carriage, staring out the side carriage windows, I knew I shouldn't have come. Why had I set myself up to walk alongside him for a stroll through the park? What was wrong with me?

I liked him more than anyone I'd ever met before, that was what was wrong with me. And there I was practically inviting him to take another chance.

And I shouldn't have wanted him to. I didn't know if I'd be able to resist giving in to him if he reverted to how very amiable he'd been the first time we'd met at Brittle Brattle Books.

On our ride to drop Sylvie off at her friend's house, while Vance and Mr. Hawthorne spoke of horses and made plans to go riding together sometime, Sylvie scooted closer to me on the bench and whispered in my ear, "Mabel told me what you overheard between Mr. Hawthorne and his friend at his house. So I think I'd better give you another lesson—"

"Really, Sylvie, I don't need any more lessons," I whispered back, though what I'd said didn't mean anything to anyone. "I've decided against everything I thought I needed help with."

"You need the lesson even more, then."

"All right. What is it?"

"Let Mr. Hawthorne court you." She made sure to cup her hand over my ear, which caught Mr. Hawthorne's attention. His gray-blue eyes met mine across the space of the carriage, even as he was in the middle of saying something to Violet.

My heart skipped as Mr. Hawthorne's ever-so-slight smirk kicked up at one side, and I drew in a quick breath.

"That sounds more like a demand than a lesson," I uttered back to Sylvie.

"And a marvelous one, if I might say so. Just imagine."

I didn't need her help imagining. Wondering what it would be like to allow Mr. Hawthorne his suit was already something I continually fought against on my own without her help in bringing up the idea. Especially when he continued to glance at me during our carriage ride throughout town.

It didn't take long to get to the park after dropping Sylvie off at her friend's house. When the carriage stopped on the east side of Riverway Park, Vance helped Violet out first. Then Mr. Hawthorne climbed out to help me. As Vance and Violet started down the path, Mr. Hawthorne offered me his arm.

I placed my hand upon his forearm until my fingers curled into the bend of his elbow. Goodness, I'd had no idea he was so solid.

I sucked in my breath, unable to refrain from thinking back to when I'd watched him in his home. How differently I'd thought of him then, how hopeful I'd been, and how thrilling it had been to study him with awestruck wonder for those few minutes before overhearing his conversation with Officer Underwood that had changed everything.

Mr. Hawthorne and I stepped down the path in silence, and I wondered again if the walk wasn't merely a terrible idea, but rather the most horrendous idea ever.

We didn't go far before he guided us off the path toward a stone bridge that went right over another path that Vance and Violet had taken. They'd already been well on their way to losing us, especially now that we'd stopped.

Trees surrounded us all along the hills that sloped up to each end of the bridge where it met the bridle path, and the green canopy of leaves overhead provided much-needed shade. The bridge he'd chosen to take me looked quite peculiar, as if it were supposed to be built over a river or canal, but instead, a dirt path went under it.

Mr. Hawthorne guided me toward the wall of the bridge and I let go of his arm. He took off his hat, holding it in his hand. "Look, I wanted to apologize for what happened when you were visiting my sister."

I didn't give him an answer, for I didn't know what to say. I didn't want to say anything. And why did he want to apologize to me? I'd been the one in the wrong.

Mr. Hawthorne smirked, then looked over his shoulder to be sure no one was near enough to hear. "I don't want you to think I blame you for being in my house…" he leaned in and continued with a whisper, "for being found in my bedchamber."

I bit my lip, tried to control my breathing, and couldn't say a thing.

"I know how May—Mabel is. She's got something of a fearless spirit, and there's no stopping her once she gets something in her head."

Having failed to answer him still, he walked me over to where a wooden door with an iron lock built was into the stone wall of the bridge, as if there were a room inside. Beside this door, banked against the hill sloping up the bridle path, stood a short stone wall just the correct height to be considered a bench. The small, discreet area created something of a private alcove.

He set his hat upon the stone bench. "I also wanted to speak with you further about the discussion you had the misfortune of overhearing."

At this subject, I was no longer able to remain silent, and turned to face him. "But I'm glad I did have the *misfortune* of hearing it, Mr. Hawthorne. It has saved me a great deal of heartache."

He looked at me long and hard at this. "Is that so?"

Too late, I realized I'd let him know a bit too much of my conflicted feelings regarding him. But then again, he likely already knew from how obviously attracted I'd behaved at the bookshop, and how differently I'd been since the day at his house. What I'd said had probably only confirmed his strong suspicions.

In an attempt to gain better control of where the conversation was headed, I turned about, paced a bit, and fiddled with the strings of my reticule. Then I sat upon the half-hidden bench abutted to the wall of the bridge, next to his top hat. "Father told me you left your previous position at his bank without a word. Is that true?"

"So you've been speaking about me to your father?" he asked, evading my question.

"Simply trying to figure out the mystery you've presented."

"Ah, a mystery. How thrilling for you."

Looking apprehensively to Mr. Hawthorne, I found him leaning against a tree, staring at me.

I couldn't help it as my gaze traveled the length of him, from his tousled brown hair, to the breadth of his shoulders, down his long, muscular legs to his fine leather shoes.

Yes, what a distractingly handsome mystery he made.

"I never knew I was so intriguing... but I'm immensely glad your thoughts of me have—"

"Not intriguing," I promptly interrupted. "Secretive. There's a difference."

"I haven't been secretive with you." His leveled gaze focused entirely on me. "You know exactly what I think of you."

"Oh yes, let me remember," I stated lightly. "You said something about me being difficult to forget. Perhaps a comment about my looks from back when I'd just come out..."

"I may have commented on your appearance years ago, but the same would be true now. You were, and *are* very beautiful. Especially when you're being inquisitive," Mr. Hawthorne said, and then he quickly pushed off the tree and raked his fingers through his hair. "May I have the chance to explain what you heard while you were eavesdropping on *my* private conversation?"

Scared of what he would actually say—and how hearing such things could possibly change my mind, make me want to give in—I said, "You needn't bother. It won't change—"

"Let me anyway, for the benefit of you knowing a little more."

"If you must, Mr. Hawthorne." I spread out the creases of my shirt.

"It will make me feel better, and I think it might do the same for you." Suddenly, he sat down beside me, took my hands in his, and turned his entire body to face me, grazing my skirts with his knee.

"Officer Philip Underwood is a friend of mine, and I do what I can in the situation I've been given to be a help to him."

That this was the part of the conversation he wanted to discuss—and not the part about his interest in me—was quite relieving, and I allowed my hands to relax in his grip. This was a much better topic, and one that would do me good to hear again.

"Oh yes, your dangerous situations, like the one in which you were shot last summer. Do tell me more about what a daring life you lead." I knew it was silly to say such things, all while letting him hold my hands.

He gently moved his hand around mine, cradling the back of my hands, curling his fingertips into my palms. Stunned, I simply stared down at our joined hands for a moment, watching as my fingers treacherously covered over his in response.

A brief, gentle smile stretched across his face at this, but when he went on, he was still quite serious. "What I do is not that dangerous, and it's also not about me. Everything we do concerning this case is for the sake of others. Others who don't even know they're in danger, and wouldn't know until it was too late."

"What do you mean? Who are you talking about?"

"Girls like a Miss Philomena Lassiter, a Miss Sadie Martindale, and even your own sister-in-law, Violet. Among many others."

"Violet?"

"You were traveling Europe last summer, of course." He squeezed my hands, but then let go, turning to face the tree-lined path again. "Of course, you have no idea."

"About what?"

"I'm not supposed to tell anyone anything about what I'm doing, and especially not speak of such things to young ladies, but you've given me no choice. Not if you're going to hold what I'm doing against me without knowing the truth of the matter." He refrained from turning to me again, and instead, he spoke to the trees. "But you need to promise me that you won't tell anyone what I'm about to tell you."

"I promise," I sighed, meaning the words from the depths of my heart.

"There's a good reason I'm working with the police. There are helpless young women being targeted by monsters of men who want to own them and use them for their own personal gain. Monsters like Violet's brother—Ezra Hawthorne—my own cousin. And because he's my cousin, and I've been in the position to help, I've been doing what I can to get close to him and his friends here in Boston. The police thought, since I was in the area and had a connection to him, I would be able to find out important information about his meetings, his friends, and his plans regarding tricking the young women to board the train north."

"Why north? What does that mean?"

"Ezra has friends of his posing as respectable couples recruiting young women to work at places like your sister-in-law's Everston or the grand hotels in Bangor, Bar Harbor, or Portland. But once kidnapped, there's no one to help them get away from the real plans, which truly have nothing to do with respectable hotels."

"Then what?" I swallowed. I wasn't sure I wanted to know.

"They're enslaved, forced to work in brothels." His words were to the point, but I understood why he'd had to tell me like that, to make the severity of the situation clear.

"And that's how...why you were shot last summer?"

"Saving those girls I mentioned—and many others—from being kidnapped and taken to the brothels servicing the many lumberjacks working the forests in the northern half of the state."

"What ever happened to the girls you saved alongside Violet?"

"They work at the Trinity School for Girls—one in the kitchen, the other as an assistant to the school nurse... but there are so many others." Mr. Hawthorne covered his left thigh with his hand and rubbed it subconsciously, and then looked at me with what almost looked like regret in his eyes...regret that he'd had to tell me so many disturbing, yet soul-stirring details concerning his cousin.

"Is that where you were shot? Your leg?"

"It is."

"But...saving young women and getting shot at, isn't that what you're normally doing?"

"Hardly."

I didn't know what to think. Of course I was happy Violet and those other young women hadn't been harmed, but why did *he* have to be so intricately involved?

He was the most remarkable man I'd ever met, and the thought of his safety, and then also the safety of the young women targeted by such vile men warred within me. I didn't want to like this—admire this—about him.

But then, how could I not? His convictions regarding his work with the case were immovable... but would not my regard for him lessen if he were less concerned for them?

"Mrs. Everstone, I think I can understand your concern for me, but please, be rest assured, I know what I'm doing. It isn't nearly as dangerous as your imagination leads you to believe."

"You merely talk with and stay in contact with your cousin?"

"That's about the extent of it."

"Violet's brother...Vance married her knowing about this awful brother of hers?"

"Yes, Vance saved her from her brother, in more ways than one."

The idea that Mr. Hawthorne's cousin, and Violet's brother, could be such a wicked man was astonishing, but I couldn't find it in me to judge her for having such a brother. And therefore, I found, his being Mr. Hawthorne's cousin had no bearing either. Vance certainly hadn't minded when he'd married Violet, and neither had his family, apparently. But I was fairly certain that Miss Abernathy wouldn't have known, or she wouldn't have been nearly as graciously accepting of Violet and her cousins, not if her views of someone like Mr. Chauncey Hawthorne III were so tainted merely by the despicable actions of his father.

"But you mentioned something about catching your cousin, a possibility of getting shot at again? There is still danger?"

"Once he's caught, it will be over. They won't want my help anymore. I am a mere civilian, after all." He stood at this point and pressed his hands together, rubbing them vigorously and then wiping them on his thighs, which made me wonder, did this conversation make him nervous? But when he continued, he didn't seem nervous, only strong and confident. He shook his head. "There are times I wish I didn't have to involve myself, but then, who would? I feel honor bound to do what I can." He darted his eyes down to me, as I still sat upon the bench staring up at him. "Is it not our Christian duty to help, even if our lives are put in danger?"

I couldn't refute that, so I said, "Helpless girls...do you mean orphans?"

"Sometimes. Other times, they are runaways or young widows without connections. Or, like in Miss Lassiter and Miss Martindale's cases, simply young woman who need a job, and think traveling north to work in a bustling resort sounds interesting. But yes, most times, they are destitute and looking for a way to survive."

"Don't events like the Charity Ball for the sake of raising money for the Children's Aid Society of Boston help?"

He laughed under his breath as he paced before me. "In its own way."

"You don't support benefits for—?"

"I didn't say that." He gave me a harsh look. "It's just that what I'm doing for the police is on a completely different level than that of the wealthy Bostonians opening their pocketbooks for the sake of keeping the orphan school funded. They cannot even be compared. They are two very different things."

I hated—and adored—that everything he did was for a deeper cause, for the benefit of those lost and alone girls on the verge of being tricked into a life of helplessness. The same girls my parents and I had always taken pride in supporting through our charitable donations to the Children's Aid Society of Boston, as well as the Boston Inland Mission Society, which housed the Trinity School for Girls. Then there was the Charity Ball. We'd always had a large role in putting those on every year, at least while we were in Boston. Not that he'd insinuated that they were useless events that didn't help…but he was right. They were two totally different things. What he did, and what I did, for ultimately the same cause.

He *was* a hero, many times over, and sacrificial and dedicated… and I…I helped plan a community event and merely shared the task of securing the items that would be donated for the silent auction with my parents. Which was basically nothing in comparison.

"Are you planning to attend the ball?" I asked.

"I am not," he answered as he again took his place against the nearest oak.

"Oh," I answered, disappointed by the fact that he might not make it. I'd expected he would. I knew his sister had plans to be there.

"Tell me, do you have a specific role concerning the Charity Ball, Mrs. Everstone? I know your parents are on the arrangement committee and were doing their duty with reaching out to the community to collect items for the silent auction, but what do you do? Are you also involved?"

"I'm not part of the committee, but I have helped with making requests for items, and I also help with the organization and setup of the silent auction at the ball."

"Then God is using you in the best way possible, for I'm certain no one is able to say no to anything you request of them." His eyes gleamed as he looked down at me.

Although he'd made the sudden switch to being flirtatious, my thoughts wandered back to what he'd asked. My part in the whole scheme of things was fairly insignificant compared to what he was willing to do for the sake of the helpless. And suddenly I realized how he must have felt when faced with the option of helping to capture his cousin, or turning his back on the entire situation.

"It isn't much, is it?"

"But you know more now. You can do more."

Could I? I wasn't so sure.

And was God using me?

I took a moment to think, realizing I had no idea how to answer this startling question.

Was it enough that I volunteered my time at charity balls and the like for the purpose of raising support and funding for organizations like the Children's Aid Society? Suddenly, it didn't seem like I did much of anything. I'd had acquaintances who had volunteered their time teaching the girls at the school once a week, but I'd always been too busy. And my mother had always seemed to think that our participating in the benefits was enough. But did she know what kinds of things were happening to these young girls, the ones who might not have the safety of the girls' school

anymore? What happened to the orphaned girls once they graduated and were forced to leave?

"Apart from the case," he went on, "and apart from being shot
last summer, there was something else my friend and I discussed
that day you were listening behind my bedchamber door...."

I knew exactly what subject he wanted to discuss now. It was
the only subject left, and I stood, ready to walk away, straight into
the park to look for Vance and Violet. But I only got as far as
standing before him, facing the tree he leaned so casually against.
His blue gaze burned with unconcealed desire, and I couldn't walk
away.

Something inside held me back, something a little too much
like *anticipation*.

I couldn't just sit down again, not with him standing there
looking at me like that. So I turned around and walked back
toward the rounded door in the wall of the bridge, hoping that
merely moving about would perhaps divert me, calm my nerves.

"Yes, Officer Underwood said something about 'the likes of
Cal Hawthorne,'" I said, grasping at any last straw of resistance I
could. "What did he mean by that?"

"I will tell you more about that if you'd like." He pushed off the
tree and took a few steps in my direction. "But you need to know:
that knowledge comes with a hefty price."

I backed up a bit and found myself standing against the stone
wall of the bridge. "I'm not *that* interested then," I lied.

"I didn't say *what* I wanted specifically."

"I can tell what you want, Mr. Hawthorne." My gaze willingly scanned his face as he continued to draw nearer, and I had to
admit, if he meant to kiss me, I wasn't nearly as disagreeable to the
notion as I should have been. In fact, I was shocked by how much
merit the idea had. Suddenly, I was unable to keep my mind off
the clear image of all of him pressed to all of me against that wall,

hidden away in the leaf-and-stone alcove, right there in the middle of Riverway Park.

When he reached me, he stood about a foot away and placed his hand against the wall above my shoulder. "It would seem you have quite the knack for reading my intentions, Mrs. Everstone. But I can assure you, they are much more complicated than what you're thinking at the moment."

"Oh, you've been quite clear about those intentions from the beginning of our acquaintance, Mr. Hawthorne."

"I can tell you're scared." He leaned over me a bit, dropping his gaze to my lips. "I want you to trust me."

Did he mean to imply my fear concerning his willingness to put himself in danger for the sake of others, or how scared I was to give in to everything I couldn't help but feel for him? Or were the two matters so intricately involved that conquering my fear of the one could dissolve the power of the other?

"Put your guard down," he whispered. "Let me in."

His words hammered at my heart, and if it weren't for everything we'd just discussed at length, I would have gladly done what he asked. If only he weren't involved in such dangerous ventures, I could let myself fall in love with him. Quite easily.

"I can't," I said, gazing into his eyes, giving away entirely too much. But as I was already well aware, it wasn't a secret I liked him much more than I ought.

"That's a fair answer, I suppose." His thumb grazed my bottom lip. "You simply can't…right now. Which is understandable."

I ducked away from the wall and walked past the tree he'd been standing against earlier. Turning, when I felt I was a safe-enough distance from him and his ability to make me want to do highly inappropriate things, I found him still leaning with his hand against the wall, just as he'd been when I'd practically let him kiss me. Only now he looked over his shoulder, the look in his eyes inscrutable.

"I must thank you for clarifying the details about what you do for the police, Mr. Hawthorne." Though I didn't have the first clue what I was going to do with the information I'd been given. I already felt that what little defense I'd had at the beginning of the outing was now toppled to the ground merely by being near him and hearing everything he'd had to say.

Letting out a long breath, Mr. Hawthorne took his hand from the wall and gathered his hat from the bench. "Well, we'd better get back to our walk. Vance and Violet should be back soon."

"Yes, I suppose they will," I replied.

A little later, after we'd picked Sylvie up from her friend's house, I was let off at Faircourt before the carriage was taken farther down the street to Everthorne. Mr. Hawthorne took it upon himself to climb out before me and help me descend the small metal steps.

He then escorted me to my parents' front door. "I hope you realize what a great pleasure it has been, my having the chance to see you again, Mrs. Everstone," he said, as my hand still rested on his arm.

"I...I..." What could I say? It hadn't all been a pleasure for me. Most of it had been an extremely difficult conversation, one that I knew he could have easily taken to a much different level...if only I'd been able to do as he asked. If I'd been able to let my guard down.

But I couldn't let myself like him.

No matter how much I did.

"I'm glad we had our conversation today," was all I ended up allowing.

He seemed to understand this was enough, for he made a bow and rang the bell. Once my parents' butler opened the massive carved-wood front door, Mr. Hawthorne took the steps down to the sidewalk. But instead of climbing back into the carriage, he tilted his hat to Vance and kept walking in the direction of Everwood.

Forcing myself to close the door as he walked away, I then ended up watching him from the front windows to see if he were indeed heading to Everwood. And he had been, for some reason.

Turning from the window and swishing the curtains back in place, I knew I shouldn't have cared. But then again, with Mr. Cal Hawthorne, doing what I should, and not doing what I shouldn't, was becoming something I couldn't quite master.

And I felt like kicking myself.

For one thing had become vividly clear during this outing to the park: No matter how I tried, there was something about him—about his every word to me—that made it impossible for me to keep the treacherous feelings he'd first induced at the bookshop tucked away. And despite what I knew of his involvement in the case concerning his rotten cousin, I cared entirely too much about Mr. Cal Hawthorne and what he thought of me.

9

Faircourt

"When a man has seen the woman whom he would have chosen
if he had intended to marry speedily, his remaining a bachelor
will usually depend on her resolution rather than on his."
—George Eliot, *Middlemarch*

During the next week, I ended up hearing more than I'd ever wanted to about Cal Hawthorne from almost everyone I spent time with. He hadn't been around in all that time though—which made the situation even more frustrating. Vance and Violet often spoke about our time at the park, which would then remind me of everything he'd said to me that day. Father would mention him haphazardly, always talking of the dinner he hoped to invite Mr. Hawthorne and his family to, though I still didn't know of plans to actually do so. And Miss Claudine Abernathy's sole purpose in life seemed to consist of getting me interested in marrying him.

She'd been trying to persuade me I needed to spend more time with him, catch his attention, and let him know how very attractive I found him, now that she'd found out I'd indeed met him and spent some time with him at Riverway Park.

All of which was unneeded.

And unappreciated.

And completely working.

It was all fairly impossible to ignore, for Mr. Cal Hawthorne had crashed into my life that day in the bookshop, and nothing had been the same since. And witnessing Father's amiable interactions with him the afternoon at Rochester Farms, combined with everything Mr. Hawthorne had explained about why he did what he did, had done some detrimental damage to the barriers I'd been trying to construct.

He was too attractive, drew me in too easily. If he was able to keep seeing me, keep trying to get to me, as he had that afternoon at the park, I didn't know what I would do. Why did he have to be so good? So perfectly heroic?

I'd meant to ask Violet about the situation when Mr. Hawthorne had saved her last summer. I also wanted to meet Miss Philomena Lassiter and Miss Sadie Martindale, the two girls who'd been saved alongside her. I knew that putting faces with those names would help make things more real for me. Whenever I recalled what kind of future they would have had, if not for Mr. Hawthorne, my admiration for him only grew.

I'd known a number of fine gentleman over the years, of course, but no one as kind and considerate and determined as Mr. Hawthorne. And then added to that, how breathtakingly handsome he was. It was such a precarious mix, and one I hadn't been able to withstand.

And yes, it all was so *dangerous*.

The word meant so many different things to me now, though.

I was afraid for so much more now, and it wasn't just concerning my own heart. I was afraid for these girls who could so easily, so innocently, be tricked and then trapped into living a nightmare.

Somehow their plight had lodged itself into my heart, so much so that when I'd thought of all Mr. Hawthorne did for them, it didn't so much scare me, but rather, made me proud.

So proud of him.

And consequently, everything he'd told me about the whole situation spurred my thoughts on to what more could be done. But every single idea I came up with didn't seem nearly enough. What could be done to equip these young women once they were released from the orphanages at the age of sixteen? How could we steer them into the right direction for employment, and direct them to places and people who weren't trying to trick them into a life of slavery?

I wasn't used to thinking in such directions, but it was quickly becoming all I ever thought about.

For if I thought of Mr. Hawthorne, I thought of these things.

Then also, if I thought of these things, I thought of Mr. Hawthorne.

And now I looked forward to seeing him again, to gain his opinion and insight on what else could possibly be done for these girls who were preyed upon by men like his cousin. How could we better guide them? Help them?

After spending the afternoon at Everwood with my mother, Miss Abernathy and Sylvie, and yet again, being unable to find the courage to bring up any of these concerns I had about the young women graduating from the orphan school, I entered the front door of Faircourt, and my parents' butler, Fellers, greeted me.

"Welcome home, Mrs. Everstone."

"Good afternoon, Fellers. Thank you."

He closed the door behind me.

"Your father has been with some visitors in the back parlor. He told me to inform him if you should arrive home while they were still here. He would have you join them."

Which was strange since Father didn't usually like visitors when he had a Saturday afternoon all to himself. Even if he did have someone over, he usually entertained his friends in his study and certainly didn't include me.

Fellers disappeared down the hall, making me feel a little as if I were a stranger in my own home, waiting to be seen by my father and his guests.

A few minutes later, Fellers came back for me. "You are welcome to join them now."

My heels sounded on the marble floor all the way down the hall to the back parlor, echoing loudly, announcing my arrival. I wondered why Fellers hadn't felt the need to inform me who exactly I was supposed to be joining in my own home. It was all very confounding, and I didn't like how secretive it all seemed.

Fellers used both hands to slide the large, seldom-used pocket door open, and it rumbled loudly as it barreled into the cavity in the wall. There was no hiding the fact that I was coming now.

When Fellers moved out of the way, I found Vance Everstone standing in the room next to my father, alongside none other than Mr. Cal Hawthorne.

I slowly stepped from the hall into the parlor, but I couldn't keep my eyes off Mr. Hawthorne. Although I strived not to seem too interested that he was there, I could tell my undeniable attraction to him radiated from me. There seemed to be nothing I could do to prevent it. Everything felt so strong, so much stronger than anything I'd ever felt before.

Mr. Hawthorne was dressed in a three-piece suit of the same level of stylishness as Vance, and the effect a simple change of clothes made was absolutely mesmerizing. He'd been clothed in fine enough suits every other time I'd seen him.

But this.

Had Mr. Hawthorne come to see me?

The thought thrilled me, and I purposefully refocused my gaze away from him.

"Ah, Nicholette." Father stepped across the room to me and took one of my hands in his. Could he tell I felt like running in the opposite direction? "You're just in time to join us for some tea."

Vance shook his head, holding up a hand in polite refusal. "I actually had my fill earlier this afternoon, thank you." He turned to shake my father's hand. "I should probably be leaving."

"Oh, already?" I couldn't help but look at Mr. Hawthorne's face, fully expecting to see his intoxicating smile. But I caught him watching me with a serious look, the weight of his thoughts evident.

"I need to get home. Violet is expecting me," Vance added, answering my question.

"I'm grateful you came, Vance, and you too, Cal." Father turned to face us as he spoke.

"It was nothing," Vance responded. "I'm glad I could come along."

"And Cal, since my daughter has just arrived home, you'll be staying a bit longer to have tea with us, won't you?"

Mr. Hawthorne caught my eye as he replied, "I'd be glad to."

"Then it's settled." It was uncharacteristic of Father to care much about being hospitable, and instead of tugging the bell pull, as Mother would have, he uttered, "Excuse me, then. I'll have tea sent in." And he left the room entirely.

"Well, I should be off." Vance exited, and Mr. Hawthorne and I followed him down the long hall to the front of the house. As Vance collected his things, I nervously fiddled with the strings of my reticule.

"It was good to see you again, Cal." Before Mr. Hawthorne could respond, Vance went on. "And I look forward to seeing how everything we spoke of today pans out."

"Me too." He uttered the words so that only I could tell what he'd said, and he'd said them so pointedly, that for a moment, I was only able to stare at him, my heart beating erratically.

Before I could respond, Vance left without further ado.

Mr. Hawthorne closed the door behind him, and we were left standing there alone, waiting for my father to rejoin us.

He would, wouldn't he?

Mr. Hawthorne smiled then, that same half-hidden—and yes, definitely intoxicating—smile from when I'd first seen him almost two months before.

When he didn't say anything, I said, "I wanted to ask you something, Mr. Hawthorne...will you be attending the dinner party at Everthorne in two weeks?"

Although there were a great many things I wanted to bring up to him regarding what we'd discussed at the park, I knew this was a safe-enough question that it wouldn't seem too intrusive for an afternoon tea, especially if my father were to join us again soon.

"I've been invited," he answered, politely.

"But you're not planning to attend?" I gracefully swiveled away from Mr. Hawthorne to walk down the hall to the back parlor where Father would be, hopefully, awaiting tea.

"As of right now, I have other plans that evening," he answered from behind me.

I stopped and turned to him. "What kind of plans?"

"Why, Mrs. Everstone, are you alluding that you're looking forward to seeing me there—that you would have me change my plans in an effort to spend more time with you?"

"Of course not." I turned back around with a huff and continued on down the hall. "I haven't the slightest interest in spending more time with you than need be," I lied. He certainly didn't need to know how entirely smitten I'd become with him since our time at the park. Goodness, I couldn't even fathom how forthright he would become if he knew.

"Oh, of course." He laughed, having entirely too much fun toying with me. "Vance has been doing his best to get me to change my plans, but I'm afraid it's something beyond my control. Mabel will be there, if that is any consolation."

"It will be nice to see her again." I entered the back parlor, and Father wasn't there. "I know she and Sylvie have become great friends of late."

Glancing at Mr. Hawthorne as he walked beside me into the parlor, I noticed that he now looked much more comfortable with the situation. Then, suddenly, he caught my gaze, and his grayish-blue eyes took on a new gleam, and my cheeks heated.

"That they have. They have much in common in being young and frivolous without a care in the world. I had a difficult time picturing you and Miss Boutilier being very close. You don't seem anything alike."

Sitting at the end of sofa, I said, "She's definitely cut from a different cloth than I—"

"As, I think, anyone would be able to tell." He sat as well, in a chair close to my end of the sofa.

It was amazing how Sylvie always seemed to have so much fun with life. And Mabel matched her so well. I'd never had a friend who fit me—not even William—the way I felt Cal Hawthorne seemed to.

When I failed to respond, he added, "But that isn't a bad thing, you know." He spoke so matter-of-factly, like he'd studied the subject at great length. Which was blush-inducing, considering the subject was me. I still refrained from speaking. I didn't know what to say to him beyond having the surging desire to ask him what kinds of things he'd discovered in his studies.

"Her effervescence is quite infectious, but oftentimes I find I prefer subtle and sensible as opposed to flighty and whimsical."

"Yes, that would be me, wouldn't—?" I covered my mouth with my fingers. "Sorry, not that you meant—"

"There's absolutely no need to apologize, Mrs. Everstone," he stated frankly. "I did mean that I prefer you. Highly prefer you, actually, over any other young woman I've ever met."

Trying in vain to regain my composure, because honestly, what was I supposed to say to that?—I said, "What was it exactly that brought you here today?"

He looked into my eyes, deeply, longingly. "Your father invited me."

"My father invited you here, along with Vance? I've noticed he has become a good friend of yours."

"We have become friends, yes. And I suppose your father wanted to have reinforcements ready."

"For what reason?" I asked, fairly confused.

"In case I needed to be persuaded to take the job your father was so good to offer me."

"Oh. Did you need to be persuaded?"

"Not at all. I happily accepted."

"When will you start your job at Father's bank?"

"It might not be for some weeks, perhaps not even until the end of August."

Standing, I walked the perimeter of the sofa to where some plant stands were situated before the twenty-foot floor-to-ceiling windows looking out to Marlborough Street. "Because you'd rather work for Mr. Rochester?"

"No, I would rather work for your father."

"Then why don't you just take the job? Start tomorrow?" I asked, genuinely curious.

"As glad as I am that you've finally decided to ask your questions of me, I must point out, you certainly do want to know everything about someone who doesn't interest you in the slightest." Mr. Hawthorne followed my example and unfolded himself from his seat. He turned to face me, not moving past the sofa. He simply watched me closely as I neared the large windows.

"You are highly…" I took a deep breath and thought twice about uttering my next word. I didn't need him to know that everything I'd ever gathered about him—as well as all I had yet to figure out—had become such a preoccupation of mine.

I *did* want to hide that from him…right?

Mr. Hawthorne took a few steps closer, around the end of the sofa, joining me, cornering me. "You can go ahead and keep the end of that sentence to yourself, Mrs. Everstone. I'm finding my imagination is doing an excellent job filling in the words you won't supply."

"Enigmatic," I admitted, in case his imagination came up with some other, more effective words, like fascinating, or mesmerizing, or impossibly handsome. "That's what I was going to say."

He took a step forward, moving his hand across the top of the wooden edge of the sofa, a few inches from mine.

Entranced by his closeness, I braced my hand a few inches from where his rested at the back of the sofa. Not that it would have any use in keeping him from coming closer—and really, did I want to keep him away?

Or was my hand resting there…waiting for his?

The thought of Mr. Hawthorne taking my hand in his softened something inside me, and instead of backing farther away, pulling my hand out of reach, I found myself taking a tiny step forward, gliding my hand forward…because, like always, his presence did something startling to my heart, every single time.

Mr. Hawthorne noticed where I'd rested my hand, and then brought those gray-blue eyes to meet mine. But he remained silent for a moment, saying nothing and everything all at once with that one knowing look. Then he whispered, "Enigmatic is an acceptable adjective."

At the clattery, squeaky-wheeled sound of the tea cart rolling down the hall, Mr. Hawthorne took a step back and combed his hand through his thick brown hair, causing it to stand in a ridiculously attractive wave. He walked out from behind the sofa, leaving me there, trying to understand what had just happened.

Twisting my fingers together nervously in front of me, I tried to shake the intense gratification I'd felt from almost having his skin against mine.

Father returned to the room then, a maid rolling in the teacart after him. "I apologize for taking so long, I got distracted by something that needed my attention. I hope you two took advantage of the time to get better acquainted."

I didn't bother to answer him or reclaim my seat on the sofa. Mr. Hawthorne and I merely remained as we were for a moment, seemingly unable to stop staring at one another.

And I didn't know how to move.

The maid arranged everything on the other side of the spacious room, and my father stayed near the cart, waiting for us to join him.

After a few moments of silence, and trying with everything in me to seem as if we'd just had a very normal discussion, I asked him with a little more strength to my voice so that my father would hear, "Would you like some tea, Mr. Hawthorne?"

"I would love some, Mrs. Everstone," he answered, his expression so adorably earnest, I had a feeling his thoughts ran along the same lines as mine.

As we walked together to the other side of the room, he spoke to my father.

I tried to remain calm, tried not to spend too much of my time gawking at Mr. Hawthorne like a schoolgirl, for he was devastatingly handsome. And even though I did this, I could tell that Mr. Hawthorne had his eyes on me through it all. He watched my every move, obviously not caring what my father thought.

And even though every single look thrilled me, the uncertainty of when I would next see him, and be able to bring up the subject of better quipping the girls, unnerved me.

Most of the tea turned out to be a blur of meaningless conversation. Mr. Hawthorne primarily spoke to my father about a number of things that didn't concern me in the least. And after perhaps half an hour, Father asked me to show our guest out while he returned to his study.

Once Mr. Hawthorne and I were again at the front door, he turned to me, his top hat in hand. He looked very much as if he were ready to leave, but I couldn't let him yet. Not now that we were finally alone without the prospect of my father rejoining us. I had so many things I wanted to ask his advice about.

"Mr. Hawthorne, I've been thinking about something—everything—you said at the park last week, and I wanted to ask... is there something more that could be done for young women who might not have the guidance needed to know where to place themselves once they've come of age? I don't know many skills myself, at least ones that would help them, but there must be something more we can do to help them from falling prey to men like Ezra Hawthorne."

"There is indeed something," he replied regarding me now with a different kind of look than he ever had before. It was something more than mere attraction, something like astonishment. "I know for a fact that something along these lines, perhaps an apprenticeship program of sorts, would be a great help to the young women looking for appropriate jobs."

"Yes, a program for the older girls, maybe to line jobs up for them as they graduate, or maybe temporarily place them in households where they could receive substantial training in different skill sets, and then also, at the same time, gain references."

"I like where your thoughts are headed, Mrs. Everstone," he stated with a wide smile. "And I think what you're saying needs to be brought to attention. I know for a fact that Dr. Wellesley from Trinity Church would be open to hearing more about this sort of thing from someone like you. What do you think about telling him more about these ideas of yours sometime?"

"Well, they're just ideas. I don't really know what to do."

"But just think, it could be the first step in seeing your ideas become an actuality. And wouldn't that be something?"

"Yes, it would." There were already knots in my stomach at the mere thought of going before anyone besides Mr. Hawthorne regarding such things, but I also knew it would have to be done in order for anything to ever become of my ideas. "I'll go…if you go with me." I smiled bashfully.

"It will need to be after my dealings with Ezra are complete, but I'll make the plans, and we'll see what happens. I'm certainly looking forward to it."

"Me too…surprisingly." Taking a deep breath, I didn't know what else to say, besides, "I don't know what Father will think if he comes back through and finds you still at the door."

"Oh, right. Though, I think he would understand my dilemma." Mr. Hawthorne seemed a little distracted as he placed his hat upon his head. "Good day to you, Mrs. Everstone."

I hadn't meant I wanted him to leave, but Mr. Hawthorne turned and stepped toward the door, his hand lingering on the handle. After a moment, he turned around again with a look in his eyes, a steady examination of me. He lifted his hat off and took a quick step, almost into me. He steadied himself with a hand cupped behind my neck, brought me close, and put his lips against mine.

He pulled away, but remained with his hand at my neck, his forehead against mine, and whispered, "You're enchanting, Nicholette. Especially when your heart is showing."

Cocking a little smile—probably at my utter willingness—he let go of me and placed his hat back atop his head. He then turned around, opened the door, revealing a downpour of rain outside, and left without another word.

I stood stunned by his forwardness—and his abruptness—and watched him disappear into the pouring rain. In a daze, I closed the door and pressed my back against the wide doorjamb.

The details about the afternoon swam through my mind. Everything he'd said, and my responses—and then that kiss.

I'd never been kissed like that before, so without warning... and all I could think or feel, suddenly, was with that kiss, he'd soundly placed a key into the lock of my heart and begun to turn it. To unlock it.

And oh, how I wanted my heart to be unlocked. By him.

Then there were his last words to me...I'd heard similar things before, many times, but never had those times meant more to me than hearing it from him. And even more so because I knew his compliment hadn't been meant merely regarding my outer appearance.

He'd meant he thought that about *all of me*.

10

The Summercourt Wedding

"A faithful friend is a strong defense;
and he that hath found him hath found a treasure."
—Louisa May Alcott

Saturday, August 5, 1893
Trinity Church, Coplen Square · Back Bay, Boston, Massachusetts

It was good for you to come." My mother gently touched the edge of my sleeve as she whispered this. She smiled, tried to convince me that what she said was the truth.

I wasn't so sure.

I'd not been to a wedding since my own, and already, though the setting was as different as could be, I wondered how I would make it through.

Glimpsing the wedding decor, which consisted of thousands of light-pink roses and large white ribbons, I couldn't deny they added just enough softness to the darkly wood-trimmed sanctuary to make for a romantic wedding atmosphere. The immaculate stained glass windows on every great wall of the sanctuary lit the room with beautiful, colorful shadows that, even in midday, made the electric lights seem dim.

My parents and I moved along in the line of guests filling the vestibule slowly, for the sanctuary was already mostly filled. The wedding was of such high profile, the church would likely be filled to capacity. However, since my parents and the Summercourts were such good friends, we would have a seat up front, no matter that we'd been a little later than planned.

And therefore, so would I.

Did anyone notice me? Did they remember coming to my wedding two years ago? And how nothing happy had come of it?

My last moments in the carriage with William came back to me: he'd been an incredibly attractive man, generous and loving... and willing to wait for my love. He'd been quite confident I would eventually fall in love with him, and honestly, I was probably well on my way, now that I thought back to our time together...

Until he was taken from me.

His death had been my undoing. The pain of going through everything my wedding day had turned into...I couldn't imagine how my heart would break if something like that ever happened to me again.

Having gone through such a tragic loss, brought so low by all of it and then forced into my depressing two-year mourning period, I'd wondered for months where God had been in all that happened. How could He have given me so much and then allowed it all to be torn to shreds? I'd had everything and was left with nothing.

Nothing but my inheritance and Fairstone, which was now Everthorne.

Suddenly, I'd had enough of the wedding.

Without answering Mother, I pulled back the next time the long line of guests moved toward the grand doors of the sanctuary. "I'll be outside." I squeezed my mother's hand. "I just need some time alone."

"Perfectly understandable, dear," was Father's reply.

And they let me go. I weaved through the throng of guests, all those people looking forward to seeing Clyde Summercourt and Bianca Worthington joyously join their lives together.

Taking the steps down to the brick-laid courtyard situated at the front of the gigantic church, I noticed there weren't too many guests behind us in the line to notice me. And regardless of their stares, I turned around the corner of the church in the direction of a small grass clearing, where there was another smaller building to the grand church—a small chapel and some other rooms referred to as the Parrish House.

A covered path lined with pillars of limestone made up the corridor connecting the two buildings and then wrapped all the way around a secret little space called the Garth Garden, which was tucked between the church and the Parrish House.

The enclosed garden was just to look at from the surrounding covered pathway and Parrish House windows, and not something to actually enjoy from within, as only a small limestone path circled through it. But there would be plenty of privacy offered at the Parrish House, since everyone else there was much more concerned about being seen than hiding away.

I hurried down the brick path toward the building and up the steps to the pillared corridor. Stone steps led to the upper level of the Parrish House and also a door to the main level, which I found unlocked. I entered and found a dark little hall with doors to both the right and the left.

Trying the one to the right, I found it also unlocked. Closing the door gently behind me, I turned to face the little room. It was small, with a fireplace along the wall and a small desk situated in front of a bay window at the end of the room, overlooking the small church garden. Finding such a cozy place was unexpected. And I didn't want to leave, to go back to see Bianca walk down the aisle in her white dress, so happy to marry Clyde.

Crossing the room to the window facing the garden, I let out a long breath. I sat in the wooden desk chair, not caring what it would do to my gown, only that I needed to collect myself adequately before returning to the crowd. And hopefully return before my parents were seated up front. I didn't need the added mortification of being escorted to the front all alone.

A glimmer of sunlight streaked through the shadowy room, falling across the desk, revealing an open Bible pushed to the far edge of the desk.

Suddenly seeing it there brought another less-traumatic memory from my wedding to mind, that of the verse I'd read that day. It had been my favorite chapter of the Bible, and one in which I'd unfortunately not recalled for some time. Not that I hadn't read my Bible in the last year. Far from it actually, but I'd always avoided going back to Psalm one-twenty-one since…since everything about my life had fallen apart.

Reaching across the desk, I pulled the Bible toward me and slowly turned to the book, feeling almost nervous, wondering if there would be the same comfort the words had provided so long ago, before that day.

I flipped through the pages until I found it, and then I stood, holding the Bible, preparing myself to read the words. I'd been taught to revere the spoken Word of God, and that if the words were read aloud, one should stand in worship.

And so, standing, facing the window overlooking the Garth Garden for its abundance of light flooding in, I read the words aloud. *"I will lift up mine eyes unto the hills, from whence cometh my help. My help cometh from the Lord, which made heaven and earth."*

But I didn't get further than that before I had to stop. I sat back on the wooden desk chair. It had seemed like a cruel joke to have that chapter read at my wedding, then have everything that had happened not an hour later fall upon me.

But now, two years later, I realized it was again everything I needed to hear.

I so desperately needed *His* help now. I wanted it more than to going to the wedding in the next building...I wanted to be done with the fear my own tragic wedding had created in me. I wanted... so much more.

Mr. Hawthorne's open request of me as we'd finished our conversation in the park echoed unceasingly through my mind. *Put your guard down. Let me in.*

Closing my eyes, I buried my face in my arms atop the desk and tried to pray. But all I could think about was Cal Hawthorne, and everything he'd done—everything he was. His passions, his directness, his determination to see things happen for the good of the helpless...they all moved my heart to want the same things. To be so much more.

Everything I knew of him, had learned from him, spurred me into feeling something startlingly new, and quite suddenly, I realized I didn't want to live like this, so terrified of the "what ifs" of my life. Not if there was so much more to do for others. Not if someone like Mr. Hawthorne was waiting, clearly ready and wanting to make me love him.

And that was precisely when I realized I wanted him more than I wanted to protect my heart from the dangers of the unknown. Ever since meeting Cal Hawthorne, my soul had yearned for his, and I couldn't seem to grasp any of the excuses I'd been telling myself for the last few months, excuses I could hardly fathom anymore.

I wanted this and so much more. Because for as much as I'd tried to fall in love with William, my feelings for him had never come anywhere close to what I felt for Cal Hawthorne, and it had happened in such a short time.

God, I'm sorry I haven't relied on You the way I should have regarding this. Please help me feel as if I can move forward. I want to be strong enough. I want to not be scared anymore. I don't want to be too scared to love him.

My courage bolstered, I lifted my head from my prayerful position. But even as I admitted my willingness to fall for Mr. Hawthorne, the thought of actually going through with it created a veritable wall between me and my moving into the sanctuary, where I would likely see him after the ceremony.

What would I say to him?

"Yes, you've been correct, I'm scared to death. And I don't know what I'm doing, but please continue on as you have been, and I promise to give in to you"?

From the sanctuary next door, the pipe organ started the deep, long musical tones of "Pachelbel's Canon." Bianca would be entering the sanctuary soon, just as I had almost exactly two years before to the same music.

Exiting the little room, I hurried down the hall and opened the door to the stone-covered pathway. The only way back into the service from where I was, without circling halfway around the church again, was to enter from the front corner of the massive sanctuary. But the pews were so tucked away nearest that door, it would be almost impossible to see the altar while seated there.

Which was perfect.

I wouldn't be seated with my parents, but at least I could say I'd attended the wedding. And as for not being noticed, it helped that the sanctuary was absolutely awe-inspiring in height, towering stories and stories over everyone's heads. No one would be paying attention to me on the outskirts of the room in such a grand place.

Before reentering the church, I took a deep breath.

I opened the tall, heavy door slowly and entered the vestibule. But from there, as I faced the tall double doors into the sanctuary, I was unable to move. Just as I'd felt when I'd been standing at the main entrance of the church, waiting to be escorted in with my parents, I was afraid of the memories coming back.

I closed my eyes and gripped the door's metal handles.

After standing like that for a few moments, I heard the rector's voice echo from the pulpit. He read something from Song of Solomon, but I didn't know what until he spoke a phrase I knew.

"I found him whom my soul loveth: I held him, and would not let him go."

Everything in me felt these words, and knew the truth.

I would not let him go.

I didn't want to let Mr. Hawthorne go. I wanted to keep trying, to find a way for my heart to heal. So I *could* be his.

I knew the essence of those chapters, and many of the quotes regarding love from Song of Solomon. William had quoted parts of it to me many times in the eleven months we'd been engaged. He'd loved me, and he couldn't wait to marry me, for me to be his in every way.

I knew this, and I knew there was an intriguing side of marriage that Mother had never had the courage to speak to me about. But William had. He hadn't wanted me to be afraid or nervous. He'd wanted me to look forward to our marriage.

And I had been. If the things he'd been able to make me feel with only a passionate kiss while we were secreted away in a back hall for a soiree was any indication, I had a feeling I would have enjoyed whatever it was a wife was supposed to feel for her husband.

God, I want what I experienced with Mr. Hawthorne during those first few minutes of our acquaintance, more than I've ever wanted anything with anyone. I want his love more than I've ever wanted anyone's love before.

Just as this prayer swept through me, I felt a bit of a release from inside my heart, as if a shell had been broken away. And within a moment, I heard the door that connected the vestibule to the covered garden pathway creak open behind me.

"I had hoped you'd come."

Turning, I found Cal Hawthorne, as handsomely dressed as ever, if not a little windswept. He'd taken off his top hat and had set it on the bench by the door by the time he'd said this. I was quite stunned to have been found by him, and I had yet to find any words when he continued.

"But I see you're still debating whether to actually attend or not."

"I am." I turned away from the door and backed up to the stone wall. "I am attending…not debating."

"I see." He walked slowly across the room and came to stand beside me. It seemed an odd reaction, as if doing so had been what he'd come there to do, to be with me instead of to see Clyde Summercourt marry Bianca Worthington. We were both terribly late for the wedding, and we should have been more focused on finding a seat than finding each other.

"Were you going in?" I kept my voice low as well, just in case we could be heard by anyone inside the sanctuary.

"Only if you are."

Now that he stood there before me, I didn't know what to do.

When I didn't answer him, he said, "It's commendable that you've come this far, and I can understand your hesitancy, but you don't have to." He took a step forward. "Have you been to a wedding since your own?"

"No." I swallowed. "But as I said, I'm trying. I wanted to—to be able to attend. Perhaps I'll be able to attend the reception with more success," I said lightheartedly, knowing deep down that it would likely be just as difficult, if not more so. "Were you planning to attend the reception, Mr. Hawthorne?"

"Unfortunately, no. I made no reservation to attend." His gaze darted to the high, beautifully designed ceiling. "This is the church you and your family attend, is it not?"

"For as long as I can remember," I said.

"It's absolutely stunning. I've been by before, but never inside."

"You should see the sanctuary."

"Is that an invitation to sit with you...at the wedding?" he asked.

"We should go in."

He smiled. "Yes. We should."

Yet, he didn't move.

And neither did I.

Now that he'd joined me in that lonely vestibule, so close to everyone else at the wedding, and yet so far removed, I decided actually being at the wedding wasn't so important after all.

And that being there with him...*was*.

11

The Garth Garden

"She had not known the weight until she felt the freedom."
—Nathaniel Hawthorne, *The Scarlet Letter*

O r maybe, we shouldn't," I wavered. Crossing the vestibule, I took steps toward a pew-like bench near the door Mr. Hawthorne had come in.

"Perhaps a walk around the garden would be a better use of our time?" He arched a brow but smiled, seeming somewhat reserved. As if he weren't sure if asking would be too much.

I picked up his top hat and held it out for him to take, trying my best to be encouraging but not too forward. I already knew how much he liked me, and he knew very well that I knew.

Mr. Hawthorne walked up to me, cautiously. I wasn't certain what I was supposed to say or do after allowing him to kiss me the last time I'd seen him. "It *would* be much more proper for us to take a walk outside than to remain here," I offered.

And what better place than strolling around the Garth Garden, in plain view of anyone walking or driving by, but still so wonderfully alone.

He took his hat from me and placed it atop his head, ready to go outside. Catching my eye again with an irresistible smile, he added, "After you."

He held the door for me and closed it behind us.

I didn't wait for him, for I was rather nervous again.

He followed me for a short distance past the darkened area of the corridor where there were no pillars, but a wall with an intricately designed opening looking down into the garden. When we reached the brightened part of the corridor, with the sun shining across the floor, spreading long morning shadows in the direction of the garden, I dove into what I felt we needed to discuss more than anything—the reason I was a widow and he a widower.

"I'd planned to be an Everstone almost my entire life, you know." I stopped around the corner of the first turn, placing my hand on the pillar there, turning to face him. "I never loved Nathan, back when I thought I would marry him, but he was my supposed future. And that was all that had mattered. However, I must not have made a favorable impression on him. He moved across the country for two years to avoid the engagement."

"Astounding. I cannot even imagine."

"When it was all said and done, it was William who wanted me," I swallowed, so nervous to be speaking such things aloud. "It had made William so happy to marry me. As I said once before, he'd been pining after me for years, even while he thought I would marry his brother."

He only stepped closer, silently. No words, just his eyes watching mine. But then he said, "It must have been torture."

"It was arranged by our parents, as everyone knows." I glanced up at him. "But he did love me."

"Of course he did." He leaned a shoulder against one of the stone pillars across the aisle from me.

My gaze darted to the high, beautifully designed and diverse rooflines of the two buildings we stood between. "We were engaged for eleven months."

"I know."

Continuing, regardless of the many questions his odd looks and comments put in my mind, I said, "It was a double wedding with a friend of mine—a family friend. She and her husband live on the coast of Connecticut now."

Thinking back on the details of my engagement and wedding so candidly, after trying not to for so long, I remembered it had actually been Daphne Hampton's second wedding. She'd been widowed years before, previously married to a gentleman from Germany. She'd moved there with him and had lived with him in a castle for a number of years before his death. He'd been quite a bit older, and she'd been just out of mourning when she'd become engaged to her second husband, someone more her age. Someone, I have a feeling, she was more in love with. I glanced up from my knotted fingers.

"Did you love William?" Mr. Hawthorne asked quietly. It was a daring question, but one I was glad he'd chosen to ask. It was one of the things I was trying to find the courage to tell him.

"I liked William. I always had. And I had wanted to marry him."

As Mr. Hawthorne slowly came up to join me at the corner pillar, I took a step back, pulling my fingers from the smooth stone. "But no, I wasn't in love with him."

I swiveled around and took a few steps to some small stones that led into the Garth Garden, which were likely for the gardener's use only. I leaned against one of the pillars next to the steps down, and Mr. Hawthorne joined me, faced me, and leaned against the other one.

"But I didn't want him to die. I would have been happy with him. I would have fallen in love with him eventually. I know I would have."

Mr. Hawthorne didn't seem to know how to respond to this, and I didn't blame him.

"And now, the merest mention of a wedding makes me ill." I stopped, in an effort to regain my courage. "There was so much blood, so much sadness and despair, and on a day that…."

"Hence your desire not to attend the wedding."

"Exactly."

When I didn't go into more detail, he asked, "Did you enjoy your time in Europe?"

"I did. It was exactly what I needed, to escape everything I knew, everything familiar." I tore my gaze from him, because honestly, I could let myself stare at him all day if I were permitted.

"I did something similar when Alice died."

"You left the country for a while?"

"Well, I left Boston for a few weeks."

"Where did you go?"

"To Nahant Island, just north of here. Stayed at the Bailey Hill Hotel. I had a lot to think about, and Boston had become too lonely."

"Was not being at the Bailey lonely as well?"

"I took my family with me."

"Your mother and sister?"

"And my father, who has since passed away."

I looked him in the eyes, waiting for him to expound. But he didn't. He just stood there, staring back at me. As if that had been more than enough information.

"I just needed not to be home. I had a house on Beacon Street at the time, and I'd recently graduated from Harvard and taken the job at your father's bank. Then I'd been married and widowed.

All of which happened—the job, the wedding, Alice's passing—within six months. Then soon after that, my father also fell ill and died."

Goodness, and I'd thought my last few years had been trying. How had he remained so strong through so much pain? Was his heart still in the process of healing, as mine seemed to be? Would they ever be wholly healed from such dramatic events?

"Since we've been speaking of William, may I ask what Alice was like?"

"Bedridden, for the most part." Mr. Hawthorne raked his fingers through his hair, messing up what his valet had probably spent an hour taming. "Like your own marriage to William Everstone, my father had made plans with an old family friend of his…like his father did before him." Mr. Hawthorne huffed, shaking his head.

"What's the matter?"

"Just the irony," he said dryly.

I didn't know what he meant, but I also felt that it wasn't something he wanted to talk about.

"Alice was only seventeen when we were married. A very young seventeen. You see, she'd been terribly ill, which was why we'd married when we did." In much the same manner as I had, when I'd been speaking about William, Mr. Hawthorne stared up at the intricate stone details of the Parrish House as he spoke. "I'd just graduated from Harvard, and she was just old enough. And as I told you once before, we were only married for three months before she passed."

"How tragic for her parents. And you."

"Honestly, now that it's all in the past, I feel as though they knew, and they were endeavoring to distance themselves from the inevitable, and giving her everything she wanted all at once."

"So Alice knew you before you were married, then? As I knew William his whole life?"

"Not quite that well, but we'd met before. She looked forward to the wedding day in a way that only a schoolgirl could. And I wasn't opposed to the marriage...to doing what I was told."

Glancing at him again, I caught Mr. Hawthorne watching me as he spoke, a serious look on his face, but as if he were indecisive about something.

"She was so idealistic, so innocent. She was much like your friend, Miss Boutilier."

"I'm sure for those last three months of her life, you were a charming husband for the poor girl."

"I tried, but it wasn't much like a marriage, if I may speak frankly."

I looked away, down at my hands. They were gripped together nervously in front of me.

"She resisted any kind of companionship when it came down to trying to get to know one another. She would shell up, cower, giggle, as if she had no idea how to speak to a man, let alone get to know a husband."

Lifting my eyes to his, I took in the ruddy glow his honesty had cost him. Did he think I would judge him? Decide I wouldn't like him enough to continue, whatever it was we were doing? Suddenly, the idea of holding his injured, hurting heart in my possession, and that he wanted me to, overwhelmed me.

"She had her room, just as it had been at her parents' house, full of her little girl things, her small canopy daybed. And she didn't want...she didn't want a *real* marriage. In all honesty, there was much more missing from the arrangement than all that. I always thought that a marriage could be based on what little friendship Alice and I had, but now...I want so much more. Like the pull between *us*."

This directness of his was one of the things I liked best about him, and hearing this much about his marriage was actually refreshing. For despite the fact that I was a widow and he was a widower, neither one of us had ever truly been married.

Glancing into the small garden, instead of at him, I realized that the wedding would likely be finished soon. I fiddled with the abundance of green ruffles attached to the skirt of my gown and turned to look toward the stone corridor we'd tarried through. "I suppose we should make our way back to—"

"Has this conversation been difficult for you to hear?" Mr. Hawthorne pushed off the pillar and met me where I stood, probably closer than he should have dared within view of the street.

"Not at all."

Trying for confidence, I circled a few inches around the pillar until I reached the outer corner of the Parrish House about a foot away, where the covered corridor continued to follow its eastern-facing wall. I leaned against the stone to better face Mr. Hawthorne and provide more privacy from the street. Still near the pillar I'd just moved from, I rested my hand against it for mere strength.

Continuing, I said, "I've been thinking about how wonderful it feels to speak openly with someone about such things. We've both come from very similar situations, and now here we are, both no longer married." I shook my head, because that didn't sound quite right. "We're still here…and we're supposed to keep living."

Mr. Hawthorne let out a long breath and brought his hand to rest against the pillar, beside mine. "I couldn't have said it better myself."

With his back to the street and the eastern still-rising sun, his features were now covered in shadow, but he sounded so serious.

Inching his fingers closer to mine, he said, "And thank you."

"For what?" I asked, and it came out hoarsely. My throat constricted, I could hardly breathe.

When his hand finally reached mine, he slid his hand beneath mine, delving his fingers steadily between and then over my knuckles with a continuous motion until they were clasped, entwined, palm-to-palm.

He stepped closer, not so much shadowed now, but half facing the sunlight. He stared down at me, taking a rather intimidating inspection. "For letting your guard down."

Was he going to kiss me again?

Goodness, I hoped so.

He pressed our joined hands to his chest, and I could feel his heartbeat beneath his jacket. It pounded heavily against my wrist. I studied our entangled fingers and then looked him in the face, unembarrassed by the calm he created in me, and sighed. "So I did."

"Because you evidently feel the same wild and undeniable connection I do." He reached for my elbow and slowly caressed its way up my arm until it rested at my shoulder.

I didn't move, only swallowed, and tried my best to control my erratic breath.

This lack of verbal response seemed to please him, for he smiled and went on. "You're not going to deny it?"

I shook my head just enough to establish a negative answer, and then added, "I don't feel like talking anymore." ·

"That makes two of us."

A thrill went through me, and I could barely breathe, let alone answer. And although he'd proven to be very good at reading me, since day one, my reactions to him didn't seem to be enough. In order to further convince him I meant *everything*, I brought a hand to rest on his shoulder and scratched my fingernails against the seam of his jacket.

That seemed to be enough encouragement, for his eyes darkened, his face inched forward, and his hand strayed from my shoulder to my neck, sending shivers down my spine. His body, his face, his hair, his smile: they were all still a bit foreign to me, but all combined into a new, irresistible territory, one I definitely wanted to explore and know better.

"Nicholette!" At the very French exclamation of my name, I turned with a jerk to see Sylvie coming from the other side of the churchyard, up the steps to the corridor. Disregarding the fact that there were no steps into the garden from that side, she traipsed along the limestone path of the Garth Garden, focused entirely on joining me. "They have sent me to find—oh! You are not alone. *Monsieur* Hawthorne."

Mr. Hawthorne had taken a few steps back when he'd heard Sylvie's voice, but it was still obvious that we'd been engaged in a pretty intense *conversation*. And neither one of us seemed to know how to answer her.

"*Mademoiselle*," Mr. Hawthorne finally uttered. "Is the wedding finished already?"

"*Oui*." Sylvie had stopped advancing toward us while still in the garden, and she now stood beside a bed of red poppies. "I am so sorry to have interrupted your...your *rendezvous*, but you had missed the wedding, and your parents were worried."

"It's quite all right, Sylvie. I will go to them now. I should have joined them a long time ago."

"But I do see why you have not."

"Yes, I suppose I became a bit distracted finding Mr. Hawthorne here, and I forgot all about the wedding going on inside. I apologize if you had to miss anything yourself."

"Oh *non*, save your worries. The bride and groom have been announced and have excused the guests, and everyone is now on their way to the reception."

Goodness, I had been gone for much longer than I'd imagined!

"It was very good to see you again, Mr. Hawthorne." I didn't know what else to say. We'd been on the cusp of...so much, and now there was Sylvie, and the wedding was over, my parents looking for me...and again I didn't know when I would see him next.

"The pleasure was all mine, Mrs. Everstone. Thank you for staying out here with me...for having this much-needed conversation. And do believe me when I tell you I cannot wait until we have a chance to finish...everything."

Despite the unanswered questions, the emotions *still* flying between us, and the giant chasm of desire for each other we seemed to have fallen into—despite everything—I still felt the calm between us.

Sylvie took a few steps toward me and grabbed my hand, pulling me into the Garth Garden beside her. "Well, we'd better join your parents. They want to leave presently. *Au revoir, Monsieur* Hawthorne."

I didn't know whether to be thankful or frustrated my time with Mr. Hawthorne had just been so quickly interrupted by Sylvie and the end of the wedding. I did know one thing though...I was immensely glad I'd come.

12

Everthorne

"I have so much, and without her it all comes to nothing."
—Johann Wolfgang von Goethe, *The Sorrows of Young Werther*

Friday, August 11, 1893 · Everthorne
Dartmouth Street, Back Bay · Boston, Massachusetts

A week later, when my parents and I had arrived at Everthorne for the dinner party I hadn't planned to attend, both Vance and Violet were in the grand entrance hall to greet their guests. We made our salutations, and I focused all of my attention on the people surrounding me, searching and hoping to see the Hawthornes. However, I quickly realized that Mr. Hawthorne was nowhere to be seen. As I swept through the hall on my way to the staircase, I resigned myself to the fact that I simply shouldn't have come. He hadn't been able to change his plans, and I still didn't know when I would see him again.

As most of the guests who'd arrived filed into the parlor, I realized I didn't feel like joining them. I had a lot to think about besides Mr. Cal Hawthorne.

Up to that point, I had tried not to notice the black-and-white checkered marble floors of Everthorne, the beautifully wallpapered walls, the immaculate wooden stairs of the house that was once mine, but it wasn't easy. And now that I was alone in the impressive great hall, I couldn't repress the memories any longer.

William had been so proud to purchase the mansion down the street from his father's Everwood, which was also diagonally across the street from my parents' mansion, Faircourt. Although it had been horrendously decorated at the time, eventually gutted before the wedding, and now currently redecorated to another's tastes, the stunning woodwork of the staircase, the paneled halls, and soaring twenty-foot ceilings were all so much the same.

From where I stood at the foot of the stairs, I could envision myself there—or at least, me in my old life. It saddened my heart to think of all that had been ripped from me since those carefree days. I studied the front door and the built-in shelves in the round-shaped alcove near the front of the house. Were those new or were they there before? I couldn't remember. We hadn't had the chance to go into the house many times, since it had mostly been in the process of being torn apart in those months before the wedding, but we had gone in enough to both fall in love with the place.

And William had done his best to make me fall in love with him.

He'd been a fervent lover, such a good kisser. And in missing him, I missed the life-together-ness I'd felt while we'd been engaged.

I wanted it all again, and what I felt with Cal Hawthorne was everything and more. I'd never experienced such a connection to anyone before, and it was difficult to explain. It was, as he'd described...wild and undeniable.

Feeling the need to simply look around and remember more about the house that was once mine, I ascended the towering staircase, tracing the elaborate railing to the landing that circled around to form a huge tunnel all the way to the roof, three stories up. At the top, embedded in the roof, was a beautiful leaded stained glass Tiffany window that lit up the entire place with dark shades of white, purple, red, and blue.

The amazing window had been my absolute favorite thing about the house, and it grieved me that I felt the need to mourn even its loss to me. From the second story landing baluster, I studied the intricately detailed leaded glass design of an orange tree with sun and leaves and white calla lily stems twisting and turning through the grass, when I heard footsteps on the stairs.

Mabel and Sylvie were ascending the steps up to me, and when they reached the landing, Mabel leaned over a tad and said lowly, looking straight at me, "This is great fun, isn't it? Not as much fun as snooping through my brother's house, but still."

"Is your brother coming tonight?" I hated how forward the question sounded, but I couldn't think of any other way to ask.

"He is."

The unexpected news that he'd changed his plans to be there sent sparks of anticipation through me.

Mabel then looped her arm through mine, and the three of us took a slow stroll down to the corner post of the railing, where we could look down together but still face one another in conversation. "But I wanted to tell you that it's odd that he did. He wasn't supposed to, you know. He had told me weeks ago he wasn't able to come and he'd already declined…but then something changed his mind."

"Ooh, what do you think that was?" Sylvie asked, laughing.

Mabel took my hand in hers and squeezed. "I am fairly certain his attendance has very much to do with you, Mrs. Everstone, if I may be so bold to say so."

"Why would you think that?" I asked, trying to keep calm. Truly, I didn't know how else to answer her. What did she know?

Sylvie laughed. "Why, indeed?"

Mabel motioned toward the front parlor. "Oh, look, there he is now. Late."

I looked down from the landing and saw her brother at the entrance of the parlor, wearing formal evening attire, of course, and looking marvelous. Blushing at the recollection of everything he and I had spoken of before we'd last parted ways, I backed away from the railing, unsure of what to do.

Mabel was already on her way down the stairs, in all likelihood, to send her brother up to me. Sylvie stayed back.

"I have a feeling you don't need my lessons anymore, but—"

"No, please. I'd love to hear it," I said quickly. I needed all the help I could get, for I certainly didn't know what I was doing.

I peeked beyond the railing. Mr. Hawthorne had noticed his sister descending the stairs, and when he glanced up, he found me watching him from the railing. He immediately excused himself from speaking with Vance and started toward the stairs, and to my surprise, took the steps two at a time.

"Well then," she said. "The lesson now is: don't be afraid."

"That's not a—"

"That's all I have," Sylvie uttered as she skittered off, passing Mr. Hawthorne at the head of the stairs with a quick nod in her determination to rejoin Mabel, and likely, her desire to get out of his way.

Mr. Hawthorne was beside me within a minute, and I prayed he wouldn't hear the thumping of my anxious heart. I didn't know how to make it stop. My chest burned at the thought of our last encounter—the trust, the closeness, the ease. It was such a strange place we'd found ourselves in, he and I. Having just met, but also having something between us that made me feel like we'd known each other forever.

He stood before me, his hand at the railing, in plain view of anyone wishing to find him.

I stepped forward, standing next to him at the baluster. "I thought there were unchangeable plans," I said with a little smile, pleased that the thought of seeing me again had apparently trumped the unchangeable.

"There were." Mr. Hawthorne moved farther down the hall.

He looked up at the massive spiraling staircase to the third story to get a better view of the rounded Tiffany window. "What an amazing window, or piece of art, rather. It's one of those stained glass windows by Louis Comfort Tiffany, is it not?"

I followed his lead, sure to stay near the railing where we could be seen. "It is."

"One gets so much more of its effects up here, compared to below." Mr. Hawthorne stopped at the foot of the staircase leading up to the third story. He still looked at the immensely tall ceiling as he asked, "Did you know the window was able to create such a prism of color? Is that why you came up here?"

"Yes, I knew. And it's part of the reason." I stood next to him, staring up at the gorgeous window. "You see, I missed it. I wanted to see everything again...because Everthorne used to be mine."

His gaze came down to me. "I wasn't aware of that."

"It was called Fairstone at the time, just a few short years ago. We combined the name Fairbanks and Everstone, in much the same way that the name Everthorne was made by combining the names Everstone and Hawthorne." Suddenly self-conscious, realizing I'd just connected our own last names as well as Vance's and Violet's maiden name, I added, "William bought it before we were married, but we never lived here, of course."

"When was the last time you were here?" he asked.

"Not since before the wedding. Vance bought it from me soon after William passed away. My parents thought it best, since we would be away for so long and it would be one less thing for us to worry about." I rambled on, but he didn't seem to mind. As if he understood I just needed to stand next to him and tell him all about the house, getting everything I'd bottled up for so long, at long last, out in the open.

"You were brave to have come."

I considered telling him that the possibility of seeing him again had been the reason I'd made it through the front door, but I couldn't seem to get the words out. "As you can tell, Vance didn't change any of the woodwork. The balconies, staircases, and paneling are all original, of course. All that is exactly as it's been since the house was built, years ago."

"It's impressive." His gaze followed the massive, carved-wood trim. "I have to admit, our family home in Westborough was one of the most elaborate houses in town, but it was nothing compared to this…and this amazing staircase. It's more like a piece of art, all on its own. Just like the Tiffany window." He glanced toward the upper ceiling of the third story, at the window again. "What do you think has changed the most?"

I remained silent for a moment, and then finally answered. "Me. I am what's been changed the most."

"How so?" He made sure to look straight into my eyes as he asked.

"This house, it was from a different life, one I've been mourning. Not just William, you see, but the life he'd made for me beside him. It was gone before I ever had it. And I haven't known what to do with myself since. I certainly didn't want to come here, but I'm glad I did. It's been good to look at it, to understand that, as much as I'd loved it, God has other things for me now."

I had a feeling he knew what I meant—that I meant him.

"Of course He does. You're still young, and you have your whole life ahead of you." He stared down at me, his dusky blue eyes fixed upon my face.

And I didn't care that he stared. I wanted him to. I felt like I could just be me again. Finally. I hadn't realized it until then, but I hadn't felt free to be myself in years. Even before my engagement to William had been formed. I'd simply been doing as I'd been told.

Quite suddenly, I had the most daring thought that I should, indeed, buy Hilldreth Manor.

I looked up at Mr. Hawthorne from this reverie, and he said, "You're such a beautiful mix of uncertainty and exquisiteness, and wisdom. I do believe I like you more now than I would have if I'd had my chance all those years ago."

When the flutters in my stomach settled, I was able to respond calmly. "It's likely very true. I probably wouldn't have given you a second thought, no matter what you looked like." My cheeks burned at my blunder. "Not that it matters what you look like, but you are, you are...."

He only smiled at my clumsily uttered half-admission, staring down at me with those beautiful blue eyes. He quipped a smile and full-out laughed at me. As only he could, it seemed. "What are you trying to say?"

"You aren't terrible to look at, you know." I strolled past him, trying my best to seem nonchalant. Because, of course he knew this. He had to.

"Nicholette," he whispered, following me down the hall. He'd said my name before, of course, but never in the way he did now. To me. For me, only.

And I didn't know what to say, for he hadn't exactly said anything. Just my name.

I stopped walking away, turned to face him.

He merely stood before me, admiring me. He didn't seem to want to say anything specifically, and I had a feeling he was waiting to see if I'd say anything else interesting, so I said, "How about you say something now...Cal?"

He crooked a little grin that I could just barely see, given the dim light from the corner of the landing where we now stood. He obviously took delight in the fact that I'd said his name. "Looking at you isn't difficult either, Nicholette, as I'm sure you are well aware."

I couldn't help but provide a little smile. Had anyone before been able to create such happiness in me with only words?

Cal—for I certainly couldn't think of him as formal sounding "Mr. Hawthorne" now— guided me toward the stairs. "It's short for O'Callaghan, if you must know."

"O'Callaghan?" I sighed, relishing the sound of his true name escaping my lips for the first time. "Is that a family name?"

He lifted his shoulders with a shrug. "Yes, a great-great-grandmother's maiden name…and it's not even the beginning of the atrociousness of my full name. A simple nickname from my middle name, that's how I came to be Cal." He chuckled, and the rich deepness of his voice making such a merry sound made something in my chest feel tight and free all at once. "What's your middle name?" he asked.

"Nicholette is my middle name," I admitted. "And I'll tell you my first name when you tell me yours."

"Well then, you have a deal." But he didn't go on.

"And what is it?" I asked, fully expecting him to tell me then and there.

"You'll have to be patient and wait for it." He tapped my nose with his finger.

Thinking nothing more of his playful game of harmless secrets—which I knew I would eventually find out someday—I asked, "Have you inquired about a meeting with Dr. Wellesley yet?"

"I brought it up to Vance, for he knows Dr. Wellesley quite well, and I thought, perhaps having him and Violet present at the meeting would help. They've both been leaning toward doing something more, as well."

"So, you're saying the meeting will be soon?"

"Not necessarily. Dr. Wellesley is currently at a convention in New York, and I still think it's best to not involve myself until Ezra has been arrested. But it shouldn't be long now."

"Oh, I see."

"I know you're disappointed, but it will happen. Things are just a little too complicated at the moment to allow for anything to go wrong. If he found out my loyalties were to helping the kinds of young women he targets, it could ruin everything."

"It does makes sense," I admitted.

Cal took a step away from me and hurriedly took his pocket watch out to check the time. I could tell the engraved gold was of the best quality to be had. Just as I leaned forward to better read the elegantly scripted engraving on the inside of the lid, he shut it with a quick snap.

"So," I said cheerily, hoping to change the subject, "should I call you O'Callaghan now, or simply Cal?"

"Oh, please use the name Cal." He leaned just close enough to hover at my ear. "And I will always call you Nicholette, no matter what your first name is. It suits you."

Just then, the grandmother clock in the hall began to chime the hour.

"Well, we should probably go down," I said as I draped my hand over his arm.

He rested a hand over mine.

Hanging on his arm as we walked down the impressive dark-paneled hall and elaborately carved staircase seemed to stave off the memories I'd struggled with earlier as I'd walked through Everthorne on my own. But as I was quickly learning, whenever I was with Cal Hawthorne, I was much more focused on the future than on the past.

For two long, prayerful years, all I'd done was think about the past.

And I wanted to be finished.

The call to dinner was announced below, and we continued to slowly make our way down the stairs together, Cal escorting me by the arm. As we came to the entrance of the parlor where the rest of the party had gathered, Alex Summercourt immediately came over and stole me away, as I knew he would since he was supposed to lead me into dinner. Once we were all gathered in the dining room, I ended up seated at the center of the table, with Alex to my right and Cal to my left.

After much dialogue regarding Vance and Violet's recent trip to Everston in Maine to see his sister Estella, her husband Dexter, and their new baby, Alex turned to me, quite pointedly, and said, "I know I've told you this already, but I simply have to say, you look absolutely fabulous tonight...as usual, of course."

It was amazing how the same comment said by both Alex and Cal, in almost the same manner, could make me feel so differently. "Thank you, Alex. It is something to get used to, not having to wear the grays and lavenders."

"Though no one could dispute that you looked just as lovely in those muted tones." Cal spoke the words to me under his breath as I faced Alex, and I could not, in good form, turn away.

Alex cleared his throat. "The shade of green you're wearing tonight suits you well."

I could tell his eyes weren't exactly focused on my dress, but at the lack thereof near my shoulders and neckline.

He continued, barely lifting his eyes. "I hated to hear that you'd left the country...and that it would be for such long time."

"As did I," Cal again added from my other side.

I desperately wanted to speak with him, but I had the feeling Alex was completely unaware of his breathy contributions to our conversation.

"I suppose it was good for you to get away, wasn't it?" Alex asked. "But you know, now that you're back, it's almost as if you hadn't left."

"I wouldn't go so far to say that..." Cal added quietly.

"Mr. Summercourt, you were living in New York City until recently, were you not?" I couldn't help but respond to his absurd remarks. I was beginning to completely agree with Sylvie's view of him—he was most definitely a snob who thought mainly of himself. "I'm sure that is the reason you feel nothing has changed. But all things have. Most drastically, in fact."

"But of course some things are different now," he said with a devilish grin, finally meeting my eyes. "You're free to marry whomever you wish now."

"Are you implying that I didn't want to marry before?" I asked, my voice low, not caring that it was rude of me to ask. It had been rude of him to bring it up in the first place.

"Of course not, but now that you're back from Europe and your mourning is complete, aren't you ready to plan your own course for the future?"

I looked across the table to where my parents sat a few seats down from each other. They had done what they thought was best for me in planning my union with William and the Everstone family, and it had been good. I could not begrudge them for wanting to make it happen. It wasn't as if anyone could have known how tragically it would end. No one would have dreamed of such horrid happenings.

"I don't believe it is all up to me, Alex. I trust that God has my future and He knows what I need."

"If you believe in things like that, I suppose." Alex rolled his eyes, as if the thought that God was involved in our lives was preposterous. "Wouldn't you rather simply choose who you would like? Someone familiar, someone who would provide the same kind of arrangement your family had made with the Everstones? You know, since you like being told what to do."

I stared at him, my disbelief rendering me speechless. Had he really just said that?

"Just imagine having a part in joining the Everstone and Fairbanks families, as well as now linking all that with the Summercourt family."

I was surprised by his indiscreetness. Everything I'd ever known about Alex Summercourt had led me to believe he knew what to say to get to a woman...but perhaps it was the whole trying-to-gain-a-wife part of the equation that threw him off. I was positive he'd never mentioned the word marriage in a conversation with me before, and here he was trying to incorporate it into his smooth—or rather, not-so-smooth—ways of trying to woo me.

Which certainly weren't working. Especially knowing his views concerning God's sovereignty...and my "following directions."

"What about you, Mr. Hawthorne?" I asked, finally able to turn away from Alex and his non-stop barrage of questions and comments. "What do you believe about such things?"

"I believe God works in the hearts of His people and works all things for the benefit of those who love Him," he answered without having to take a moment to think. Then he added with a whispered smile, "And I also believe that Mr. Summercourt's efforts to seek your favor are failing quite miserably."

"They are. Quite miserably, indeed." I laughed under my breath.

"And how are mine doing?"

"Your what, exactly?" I asked slowly, keeping my voice low and my eyes discreetly focused on his.

He held my gaze and dipped his spoon into his bowl of rice pudding. "My own efforts."

"Nonexistent, in fact," I answered playfully, knowing full well that wasn't the truth.

His only answer at first was that half smile he loved to playfully display, his eyes saying so much more than his words. "Is that a fact?"

"You must try harder, it would seem."

"Duly noted, Mrs. Everstone." He flashed that heavenly smile of his, catching my eye with a meaning-filled glance.

"Nicholette, it seems you've lost your chance at buying Hilldreth, as I wished," Miss Abernathy said from across the wide table. "And with the house sold, I'll be on my way to Everston to be with Estella and Dexter before we know it."

"What? Someone's bought it already? How would anyone have even known?" It wasn't as if she'd actually advertised her intentions.

"It seems someone got word of my wishes to move and they've sent a lawyer straight to Whidbey Island to speak to Nathan and Amaryllis firsthand about an offer. And they've accepted!"

"What?" I repeated, wishing I'd realized I wanted Hilldreth sooner than that evening when I'd been speaking with Cal on the landing. I looked to him now. He watched me closely, but he had a fairly indecipherable look on his face.

"And you'll never believe from whom!" Miss Abernathy loved to share news, and she did so now with a flair of entertainment. "I just found out today, but the offer was from none other than Mr. Chauncey Hawthorne III."

"What?" It was the only word I could seem to come up with after so many new and wild pieces of information came to light. And my heart sank, even as the fact that this scandalous stranger I'd heard so much about in the last few weeks became more real than ever before. How odd it was that *he* would be the one to steal Hilldreth right out from under my nose.

"Of course, Nathan and Amaryllis know nothing of the family's reputation, but can you imagine it now? Hilldreth in the hands of *those* Hawthornes? It hurts my heart to think that my decisions have come to this. For if the son is to move back to Boston, surely he'll bring the rest of his family to live on the prominent corner of Commonwealth and Berkeley...." Miss Abernathy's attention was down the table now, as she added, "I don't even know what to say."

I could hardly come up with anything myself.

"You weren't seriously considering buying it, were you, Nicholette?" Miss Abernathy asked as her gaze came back to our part of the table and fixated on me.

I looked her way. Up until that moment, I'd been concentrating on the table settings, in complete shock. "I had thought about it, a little," I admitted.

"If I'd known as much," Miss Abernathy continued, "I would have surely sent them word not to consider any offers until they heard from you. And now, how I wished I'd told them!—that they wouldn't have sold it to *this* family. I thought it was all my own wishful thinking."

And that's all it ever would be now, my heart cried. I didn't know why it mattered so much, but I couldn't fathom living anywhere apart from my parents except for somewhere familiar. Just as Everthorne would have been.

At that precise moment, Vance and Violet stood from their seats at the ends of the table, indicating dinner was over.

After everyone left the table and mingled for a while, the gentlemen of the party congregated at the far end of the dining room, and the ladies filed out to the hall. Cal caught my eye and held my gaze for a moment before I followed his sister. I stopped near him, and he quickly whispered, "There's something I need to tell you before we join the others."

"Meet me in the receiving room at the front of the house," I said as quietly as possible.

After leaving the dining room, I held back as Violet, Mother, Miss Abernathy, Sylvie, and Mabel all went into the music room, and then I walked past the curtained-off entrance of the room, down the hall, and into the receiving room. I hoped no one would notice just how long I'd be gone before rejoining them.

The small, round room I'd told Cal to meet me in was more like an alcove, with an impressive fireplace facing the doorway, which was flanked by two windows, and then as the wall curved around, two built-in bookcases. And at the center of the room was a triangular-shaped, gray Borne Settee with three seats.

I never had understood why the room had been built into the floor plan off the hall. It was a bit removed, and just out of the way enough for some privacy. But I was thankful for it now, because it was exactly what I needed.

13

After

"Each time you happen to me all over again."
—Edith Wharton, *The Age of Innocence*

I wasn't sure what to do as my hopeless thoughts regarding Hilldreth swirled about my mind. I certainly hadn't thought there would be a race to make an offer, and now it was too late.

Awaiting Cal after dinner, I opted to stand before the locked glass doors of the built-in bookcase, between the fireplace and one of the windows, studying Violet's collection of first-edition Jane Austen and Brontë novels, which I'd heard about from Miss Abernathy.

The beginning strains of Mozart's "Eine kleine Nachtmusik" came from the music room, and I realized Mabel and Sylvie were performing the piano duet they'd spent time perfecting. They both played wonderfully, and I regretted not having the chance to watch them do so. I delighted in watching others perform the piano, because I certainly couldn't. At least as not as well as either of them could.

A few minutes later, when Cal finally came to the entrance of the receiving room, he leaned against the wood trim outlining the opening, pushing the brown-velvet curtains behind him with his shoulder. "A little night music for accompaniment. How perfect." He watched me from across the room.

Laughing to myself, I recalled Sylvie's literal English translation of the German title. She always referred to it as "A Little Night Music," but always emphasized the word "little" instead of "night."

"They are becoming quite good, aren't they?"

"They do practice almost every other day, I've heard." Cal's blue eyes stayed on me as he crossed the room.

Taking a few steps away from the bookcase, following the curved wall of the round room past the window, I met him halfway. As I stood before him, he put his hands at my shoulders, holding me at arms' length, as if he didn't trust himself to touch me beyond holding me in place.

But it was already too much. Too much for there not to be more.

Reaching up, I put my hands upon his arms and pulled him nearer, making him take a step closer. Quickly, my hands were at his shoulders, and all I wanted was to be tangled up in his arms. Cal took yet another step closer and brought a hand to the back of my neck, his thumb grazing my jaw.

He swallowed nervously, which I found to be incredibly endearing. It amazed me that I could make a man of such caliber anxious. Grabbing the material of his jacket, I took a step back to stand against the wall behind me, and he followed, keeping his hands on me.

He raked his other against my side, and just as I was about to lose all patience and pull him near, he leaned forward, wrapped his arms around me, and closed the distance between us...

Pressed against him, in his arms, we were so close that my nose was an inch from his jaw, close enough that kissing him would have been extremely easy. I'd never wanted something so desperately before, and it still felt so terrifyingly new.

He looked me in the eyes and said, "I wanted to tell you how long—how very long I've wanted this. You, how long I've wanted you...how I've loved you."

Astonished by this admission, I watched as Cal's gaze roved over my features, studying me. He smiled, apparently delighted that I couldn't seem to find any words. And before I could catch my breath, he kissed me.

I closed my eyes, and his last words echoed through my mind, creating pure bliss mixed with an almost sinking feeling as I kissed him back. Lifting onto my tiptoes, I slipped my hands up his chest to his shoulders, and then slowly, to the back of his high white collar, wanting him to know I felt everything he did too.

For I certainly wasn't going to stop kissing him in order to say so.

Cal cradled my jaw, inched his fingers near my ear and then into my hair, and I sank further. He took his time, slowly, deliberately, tilting his head, and mine, in order to kiss me more deeply. The delighted sigh, which escaped his throat as he did so, sent a shiver of pleasure through me.

I raked my fingers under the lining of his waistcoat, spreading my fingers wide as they reached his shoulders.

Cal shuddered noticeably, but kept his focus on me—on kissing me—and pulled me closer. His hands pressed at my back, and yet I stayed pushed against the wall.

"Nick...Nicky..." his raspy, whispered plea brushed against my lips, and I couldn't help but smile as his shoulders still trembled under my touch.

Scrambling for a cohesive thought, I sighed. "I thought you were"—stopping to catch my breath, I eventually went on—"going to call me Nicholette...always."

"I couldn't," he breathed heavily. "I'm sorry, I simply couldn't think."

"Well, I can't hold that against you," I whispered.

I wasn't so certain how much thinking I'd been doing myself.

Cal stared down into my eyes with the biggest smile I'd ever witnessed from him spread across his face. His hand caressed my elbow, then my upper arm, and then where the ruffled edge of my gown came to my shoulder. He grasped the edge of the silky green material in his fist for a moment, then his fingertips swept against my bare skin. And now, now that so many things had been revealed between us, I felt that even our hands weren't close enough—for how close we needed to be.

And it was all much more than I could stand. Without closing my eyes this time, I wrapped my arms around his neck and kissed him again.

This time, he seemed more serious, more determined.

All of the new feelings, which had raged through me at the mere thought of him up until then, had been surprising enough, but I hardly knew how to reconcile everything coursing through me—the emotions, what he'd said, and my complete lack of regret.

I wanted him. All of him. Forever.

I'd known what it was like to kiss William in the back halls of soirees and dinner parties, but doing so with Cal Hawthorne was proving to be astoundingly different, on so many levels. And I didn't know why that surprised me, for I'd merely liked William enough to agree to marry him because my parents had wanted me to....

But Cal Hawthorne, I didn't just like him.

And I definitely *wanted* to marry him.

I was in love with him.

The piano music from down the hall ended, and everything suddenly seemed so quiet, so revered.

A thought occurred to me through the haze of desire we'd found ourselves enveloped in, and I tore myself away from Cal. "Do you mean you've wanted me ever since we were introduced at the bookshop?" We still had our arms tangled around each other, for I couldn't actually tear myself away from all of him. Just the kiss, so we could talk. Face to face. "That wasn't too long ago, considering."

"No, we'd met before that day." He glanced at the opening of the room and seemed to think it a good idea to refrain from standing against each other as we were, for he promptly took his arms from around me and guided me to sit upon the nearest seat of the Borne Settee. He then sat to my left, and given the nature of the piece of furniture, we faced each other easily, our knees touching. "Upon meeting you at Brittle Brattle Books, it was obvious you didn't remember meeting me, which wasn't too surprising."

"Why would that be?" I looked to my hands now knotted in my lap, trying to remember that day. Yes, there had been a glimpse of a memory, but nothing I'd fully recalled of him.

I looked up to face him again and startled at the intensity with which he'd been staring at me while I'd been focused on my lap.

The music from the other room suddenly picked up again. This time, it was Violet singing "Hazel Dell," an old song I knew well because it had always been one of my mother's favorites.

"You had the arrangement with the Everstones, and that, apparently, was all that mattered to you back then."

Although what he said was true, I wondered how I had ever come into contact with Cal Hawthorne all those years ago and not been branded with the memory of him for the rest of my life. "When did this happen?"

"Let's see, it was over a year before you'd officially become engaged to William Everstone." Circling his arm around the small wooden finial at the center of the back-to-back seats of the settee, Cal reached to where my gown dipped off my shoulder again. He grazed the bare skin of my shoulder, my collarbone, with his fingertips. I leaned in slightly, offering my acceptance, of every-thing. "I'd met you seven months after Alice had passed. You were eighteen, stunning, beguiling...and also my employer's daughter."

"But you were like a son to him. Father told me." Everything my father had ever said about him came to mind. If he had been like a son once, Father's opinion of him back then was surely just as favorable as it was now. But then again, there had been all the other determining factors, like the Everstones and Mother's grand wish to see me married to one of her dearest friend's sons.

"Your father knew everything, all about the sad excuse my marriage to Alice had been." His fingers had reached my neck now, the palm of his hand splayed over my bare shoulder. "I didn't know what he would think, so I'd harbored my interest, hid my feel-ings for months. And because I'd not been aware of your eventual engagement, I just *knew* you were the only young lady I wanted."

I didn't know what to say. This surprised me, yet it made per-fect sense. It was no wonder I'd felt something between us the first instant I'd seen him. There had been so much there already with-out my knowledge.

"I'd done what my father had wanted and married Alice, and I was ready to marry for reasons of my own. I wanted to marry for love, and I wanted to marry you."

Reaching my arm around the finial, I could tell he thought, at first, that I meant to stop his touch, but instead of removing his hand from my shoulder, my fingers glided along the sleeve of his jacket, on past his forearm to his elbow and up, where I gripped the back of his arm, pulling him nearer so that his hand reached behind my neck.

He drew in a slow breath and exhaled, then continued slowly. "I finally had the courage to ask for permission to court you five months later, but your father regretted to tell me you were already spoken for, and by whom."

"What did Father think?" I asked, truly curious.

"He told me about the arrangement, that it had been your mother's wish to see you marry into the Everstone family. He also told me that if it had been up to him, he would have gladly given me permission."

"Is that right?" I'd had my suspicions about my father's hopes concerning Cal and me, but this information made everything fit into place.

"My family was—is—well respected in Westborough, and my references were stellar, but you were already taken. And that was all there was to it."

"And I became engaged to William."

"I tried to forget you. But years later, I still hadn't found anyone who intrigued me half as much as you. Then one day, I heard the news." He shook his head at what had probably been a shocking, unexpected revelation. "I could hardly believe…"

"How quickly my marriage had ended."

"And that you and your parents had traveled to Europe with plans to be there throughout your mourning period." Cal slid his hand from my shoulder and stood, leaving me upon the settee. He strolled to the fireplace and rested an elbow against the mantle, as if he'd had the sudden idea that putting some distance between us was the best idea in the world. "But by then my father had passed away, and so much about my life had changed."

"So you weren't waiting for my return from Europe?" I asked, hoping to get so many more answers than the one to the question I'd voiced.

"I didn't have much hope, living in South Boston as we were, and working for Rochester… essentially hiding in obscurity because…because of the case. I wasn't quite in the position to court an heiress."

"What do you mean?" I stood, joining him before the fireplace. "Here you are, doing just that. What changed your thinking?"

"Through some act of Providence, my one and only respectable cousin in the world, whom I'd never met, came to marry into the very same affluent family you had. And then there you were in the bookshop."

Cal still had his elbow resting upon the mantle, but he allowed me to come close, to stand directly before him, close enough to touch. But he didn't move. Only watched me, studied me as I stood so very close.

"I hadn't heard you were back, for I truly hadn't kept up with the Everstones all that much beyond Vance and Violet. And after not seeing you for so many formative years, it took me a moment to realize it was you. You were even more beautiful, and so flustered by me." He glanced down, smiling sheepishly. "I certainly wasn't expecting that."

"You could tell, could you?" I laughed, a deep throaty sound I hardly recognized. When had been the last time I'd felt such joy that laughter literally spilled from me? I couldn't remember.

"I hadn't planned on pursuing you yet. But then I kept seeing you, without even trying. And then you arrived home to Faircourt the very day I'd given up trying to resist—mere minutes after I'd made my request to court you for a second time."

"You did? Was that your true purpose for that visit? But you said my father offered you your old job that day."

"The job was the reason I was there, initially, and by his invitation. But I found I simply couldn't leave his presence before knowing his stance. Although he'd been encouraging enough, I needed to know, for certain, if he would still welcome my pursuit of you."

"And what did he say exactly?"

"He said he'd long been praying for the day I would ask again."

Laughter floated down the hall to us as we heard the gentlemen leave the dining room on their way to the music room. Which meant we didn't have much time left to continue our private conversation.

"So what does all this mean? Is it still probable that I won't see you for a number of weeks?"

"Beyond my efforts to be here, probably not for a few weeks. I try to keep a low profile, but you're making it a bit more difficult than usual." He leaned over me perfectly, so I stretched my arms over his shoulders, curling one around his neck, while the other roamed from his jacket to his white collar and on up to his neck. The feel of his jaw at my fingertips sent shivers through me, and my breath hitched in my chest.

"Being here tonight isn't quite keeping my cover, but Vance let me sneak in using the servants' entrance, which is why I was late." He brought a hand to my jaw, mimicking me, and just as it seemed as if he were going to kiss me again, he merely kissed my nose and said, "We should probably join the others."

I took my arms from around him, brought my hands to my sides, and stepped closer to the same glass cabinet I'd been studying earlier. I was therefore a good distance from Cal when Vance walked into the receiving room.

"I thought you'd be around here somewhere, together." He quipped a smile at me as he crossed the room. But was he talking to me or Cal? Showing Cal an envelope, he said, "This was brought by messenger to the back door. I suppose it's something urgent."

He walked past me and handed Cal the message.

From behind me, I heard Cal open the envelope and huff out his breath.

And I knew just what the urgent message likely pertained to.

Ezra Hawthorne.

I still didn't especially like it, but as he'd told me, it would be for only a few more weeks. And then he'd never need to be so closely involved with such dangerous people again.

He was only keeping up the act of befriending an estranged cousin, after all. And for only a short time now.

After pocketing the missive, Cal turned to me with the slightest smile, as if whatever had been written in the message had changed his attitude considerably. He offered me his arm, and I took it and walked out of the room with him, following Vance.

"I'll escort you to the rest of the party, but I need to go." His voice was different now, so serious.

"All right," I said, quite surprised by the peace I found in letting him go, and to heaven only knew what kind of situation. "I'll pray for you."

"That means the world to me, thank you." Cal took my hand and gave it a short squeeze before letting go. "This situation needs so many prayers."

As I walked into the music room alone while Vance showed Cal to the back door, I began praying then and there. It wasn't the first time I'd prayed for him and his obligation to see his cousin captured; however, now it all felt so much closer.

If something happened to Cal now, I didn't know how my heart would take it.

14

The Charity Ball

"The emerging woman...will be strong-minded,
strong-hearted, strong-souled, and strong-bodied...
strength and beauty must go together."
—Louisa May Alcott, *An Old-Fashioned Girl*

Saturday, August 19, 1893 · Cravenfeld
Commonwealth Avenue · Back Bay, Boston, Massachusetts

About a week later, my parents and I arrived early at Dr.
and Mrs. Cravens' mansion for the Charity Ball, as it was
our task to direct the setup of the gallery in which the silent auction items would be showcased. There were so many great items
we'd procured from the socialites of Boston's high society, many of
them long-time friends of my parents.

They consisted of fine paintings, furniture, rare bottles of
wine, a set of Louis Vuitton luggage, a box of Cuban cigars, fine
jewelry, Champion Bloodline horses, a year of flower deliveries, as
well as many vacation stays at resorts like Bailey Hill and Everston,
donated by Bram Everstone.

Before long, my part overseeing the setup of the valuable items
to be silently bid upon was complete. The gallery looked fabulous,

and I could already tell about how much each item would likely gain for the charity, after taking part in such things for so long.

I didn't know why I'd ever thought Cal would come to something like the Charity Ball, back when I'd asked if he would be coming. I thought of our discussion about the ball, when he'd told me everything about why he did what he did for the police case. He hadn't sounded very impressed by the fact that so many of the wealthiest families in Boston merely opened their pocketbook every so often in their noble quest to help the poor, needy, and hungry children of their city, when there was so much else that needed to be done.

But soon, those much-needed donations made through the silent auction would be added up, and no matter that it was a completely different way of helping than what Cal did, it *was* helping. Although what Cal did for the sake of helping young girls being preyed upon by lecherous men like Ezra Hawthorne was much more dangerous, and heroic, this was also something meaningful in its own right. After the benefit, we would be able to give the Children's Aid Society thousands of dollars, money that would keep the many orphanages in town open and running and the children fed and clothed.

Until they graduated, at least.

But we would be changing that soon.

We would have our meeting with Dr. Wellesley, and we would make a difference in the lives of those girls who needed our help so desperately.

As I wandered around the quickly filling ballroom, I found myself wishing Cal were there. I hadn't seen him or heard from him since he'd left the dinner party at Everthorne much too early, and after all that kissing, beyond a secret note sent to me through Violet. He'd written me simply to tell me that the case was indeed in the process of being finished. I wasn't certain what that meant, but it made me hopeful that Cal would be able to come around more now that he wouldn't have to devote so much of his spare time to his cousin.

I still didn't like thinking about the kinds of dangerous people he'd had to deal with because of his cousin's wicked schemes or imagining what kind of situation it had been that Officer Underwood had needed to send for him so late in the evening. Whenever I found myself wondering too much, I turned it over to prayer. Because it was the only thing I could do.

Well, besides being at the Charity Ball, doing my part.

Which was so little.

With nothing left to do concerning the silent auction, I made my way to the entrance of the ballroom, where many of the invited elite had already congregated. Boston's finest would be in attendance that night, and it would also be my first large social event since William's death. Which meant that it had been over two years since I'd danced. I didn't plan to do any dancing that evening since Cal wouldn't be there. I hated the thought of dancing with any of the gentlemen I knew had their eye out for me since my mourning period had ended.

Declining a dance card, I instead took one of the pamphlets with the descriptions of the items being auctioned off, merely to have something to hold as I walked around.

Soon, Bram and Evangeline Everstone walked into the room, followed by both Sylvie and Miss Claudine Abernathy. I made my way to them, since they were the closest friends I had anymore.

Sylvie came up to me but then hurried me away from the rest of our group.

"Oh, I have the most delightful lesson for you tonight."

"It's all right, Sylvie. I don't think I'm in need of any more lessons since the last—"

"Let me finish, *s'il vous plaît*. I do believe you may need this lesson most of all."

"If you think so."

"My last lesson is this: forgive the unexpected. And love him anyway."

This seemed a very odd lesson, and I didn't quite know how to respond. And before I could, the Charity Ball committee chairman stood on stage in front of the orchestra. Before he even said a word, Sylvie flitted off toward a group of young ladies more her age.

"And now, ladies and gentlemen," the chairman's voice thundered over the crowd. "I have the honor of announcing some of the first special gift donations to come in for the benefit of the Children's Aid Society. The first of which is a hefty five thousand dollars, given by Mr. Chauncey Hawthorne III, in living honor of his mother, Mrs. Charlotte Hawthorne."

The crowd gasped—and I could imagine why! When had this gentleman decided to return to Boston? And before the rumors surrounding his family had completely died down? Before the legalities of purchasing Hilldreth Manor were finalized?

But then another concern came to mind—the thought of my own name and donation being announced soon, for it seemed so very egocentric. Why did we announce who and how much? Was it not enough that we were there with the goal of giving as much as we felt was needed?

I'd never actually donated to the cause before, until now. I'd always been under the wing of my parents, and then far removed from everything while we were in Europe. Now that I was home, and I had my own fortune, and my own place in society as William Everstone's wealthy widow, I'd be able to do my part. I could do more than just witness the fundraising event I'd grown up hearing all about, and eventually participating in, my entire life.

I would have preferred to have merely won one of the auctions, rather than make a special gift, but because we'd had a part overseeing the silent auction, my parents and I were not allowed to bid on any of the items.

Just as I excused myself from my parents' crowd of friends—in order to ask that my donation not be made public—Miss Claudine Abernathy walked up to me, using her cane freely.

"Did you just hear that the elusive Mr. Chauncey Hawthorne III has dared come to our Charity Ball?" she stated, her white brows bunched forward and her lips pursed. "He couldn't have been invited! Even for all his Great Uncle Perceval's money and his family's tidied-up reputation. He shouldn't have come."

"Perhaps he simply wanted to donate to a good cause," I answered what I thought was a nonsensical, silly way to look at the gentleman's willingness to face the crowds of, in my opinion, too-judgmental socialites, in order to give funds to the Children's Society. "We can't very well condemn him whilst he's being so very... good."

Personally, I thought all the prejudice against that particular Hawthorne family was a bit unfounded. Everything I'd heard about Mr. Chauncey Hawthorne II and what he'd done to his rightful heirs and widow upon his death broke my heart for the family, whoever they were.

My only real concern with Mr. Chauncey Hawthorne III now was that he had bought Hilldreth Manor, and that I, therefore, could not.

"Oh certainly, he has the money now, Nicholette. But the thought!"

"Who exactly is this Mr. Chauncey Hawthorne III fellow everyone's been constantly speculating about anyway?" I asked, hoping Miss Abernathy might be willing to share as she usually did.

"Well, the first Chauncey Hawthorne, at least, was a respectable fellow. He was particularly responsible for bringing the railroad through Westborough and much of Massachusetts during the twenties. However, the family has not been in good standing for the last few years," she stated. "Chauncey III was in Boston for some years before the scandal, as he'd graduated from Harvard, and had married."

"Yes, I'd heard he lived somewhere in Back Bay at the time," I contributed.

"No... now that I think about it, I believe they resided somewhere along Beacon Street."

"Oh, really?" Quite suddenly, I thought back to how Cal had told me he'd lived on Beacon Street while he'd been married to Alice. But I shook the thought away. A great many gentlemen graduated from Harvard, got married, and moved to Beacon Hill and Back Bay. They were the fashionable neighborhoods to live in, after all.

Miss Abernathy wrapped her free hand about my arm and guided me through the crowd, whispering. "You've heard of the scandal concerning his father, of course. After that, the son took the family and virtually disappeared for years. The family as a whole was very affluent, at least, before the scandal."

"Are they really so disgraceful? I've heard the rumors, but how could they be blamed for what the father did to cause such unfortunate events?"

"It is the way things are, dear. I cannot believe he's here now, taking part in our society, completely disregarding what everyone knows about his shameful father." Miss Abernathy led me near the refreshment tables, where she let go of me and took up a glass of champagne. "The family will be judged ruthlessly, shamed by having such a despicably wicked patriarch." She took a sip.

"What about the great uncle's will...has that done nothing for them? I'd heard that he—"

"Money isn't everything, Nicholette, especially these days."

"Do his efforts to rectify the family's name mean nothing, then?"

"It means that *those* Hawthornes can quite easily afford Hilldreth Manor now, and that's all it means." She finished her glass of champagne and moved on down the table to pick up a dessert pastry. "Yes, yes, it was a noble quest, but I'm afraid it will take more than money to restore the dignity of the name Chauncey Hawthorne. It will take the acceptance from more than one of Boston's most influential families."

I directed my attention to the dessert options upon the table, a little afraid of what she would have to say to my next comment. "You mean, *our* families?"

Miss Abernathy turned to me, stared at me until I was forced to look at her. "Nicholette, though I do realize it might seem like a thrilling prospect in an effort to bring about a little more excitement to your life, I will not have you befriending Chauncey Hawthorne III, or his sister—"

"Chauncey Hawthorne has a sister?" I asked, caught off guard. No one had exactly mentioned a sister before, only that there were legitimate children bearing their father's shame.

"Yes, though her name is still escaping me. Though, after hearing his mother's name mentioned with his donation, it's started to jog my memory. But you see, don't you, Nicholette, how they ran away, rather than stay and stand up for themselves? They must have been somewhat to blame for what happened, or why would they disappear?"

"Why criticize them for disappearing?" I asked.

I for one couldn't, for I'd done the very same thing, after all.

After William's murder, which it seemed everyone had known all about because of the newspapers, I had run away, too. Yes, it had been under the guise of my parents' wanting to take me, but it had been done because I'd begged them, crying, desperate to never see anyone I'd known ever again. I'd just wanted to be done with everything.

"Oh, it was... oh, that's right—Maybelle Hawthorne."

Maybelle? Didn't Miss Abernathy think it conspicuous that the name was so similar to Cal's sister, Mabel Hawthorne? And hadn't Cal referred to Mabel as "May" almost every time I'd heard him mention her?

Oh no.

But Cal couldn't be Chauncey Hawthorne III. Wouldn't too many of my acquaintances have known? Vance and Violet? Wouldn't Mabel have accidentally said something? She usually said practically everything that came to her mind. But then I thought back to her mention of Cal's valet and how she'd uttered something about making a mistake in saying anything about it.

I looked through the crowd to where my parents stood together, laughing, sharing their refreshments as their closest friends stood around. My mother obviously had never known a thing, for I recalled her naïveté in mentioning both gentlemen during the discussion I'd overheard at Everwood.

But Father?

If my suspicions were correct, why hadn't he told me? When I had asked my questions, he'd shut me out, told me I needed to ask Cal himself if I had questions.

Instead, I'd promptly become so infatuated with the man, I'd forgotten to even care about the answers.

Then there was Miss Abernathy, who stood before me now. Cal's mother, Letty Hawthorne, was one of her best of friends. Could Letty be short for Charlotte? Could her very own friend, in actuality, be someone she unknowingly held such severe judgments against?

And if it were all true, what would Miss Abernathy do when she found out?

"You said Mr. Chauncey Hawthorne III is now still one of New England's most eligible bachelors, despite the scandal...but that he'd once been married?" I asked, for everything in me now worked on the suspicion that we could very well be talking about Cal, Mabel, and Letty Hawthorne. And the thought that Miss Abernathy, and possibly my own mother and her other influential friends, would retain such judgments over them, created what felt like a tunnel of despair spiraling through my chest.

"Oh yes, his fortune alone will ensure he will marry well, as he had the first time. Not to anyone of our class, of course, but to someone with a good family name, but who might be, for whatever reason, in desperate need of money. Someone who wants the privilege of living in house like Hilldreth Manor."

"And his first wife…what happened to her?" I asked.

"His first wife died shortly before the whole scandal with his father came about, poor dear. I don't recall her name, though. It's a miracle I recalled the name of his sister."

"And he lived with his wife for a short while, before she passed away…on Beacon Street?" I endeavored to ask evenly, for my thoughts were fragmenting through me, sinking into my stomach…making me feel ill. Everything in me wanted to run for the door, to search the place for the familiar face I *knew* would be in that crowd…the familiar face with a new name.

"Yes, that was what I said."

In that instant, I had a most brilliant thought, the one question that would answer everything, if only Miss Abernathy could recall one more detail. "Miss Abernathy, you don't happen to remember Mr. Chauncey Hawthorne III's middle name, by chance, do you?"

"Well, of course! Everyone who's anyone from Westborough knows that. The middle name is after a great-grandmother, if I recall, and is O'Callaghan."

Although the suspect details had been aligning for some minutes, the utter shock of realizing the truth still stunned me.

Chauncey O'Callaghan Hawthorne III was Cal.

Cal was Chauncey O'Callaghan Hawthorne III.

Why hadn't anyone told me—least of all, Cal?

And what exactly did this mean?

That he, and so many other people, had lied and lied and lied.

But the more I thought about it, did it even matter?

I couldn't blame Cal for living in hiding because of the scandal attached to his otherwise good family, in South Boston of all places. I'd been guilty of hiding away myself for the last two years. And his mother and sister, perhaps it was best they had moved to South Boston and lived in their finely appointed little double house, waiting for the rumors to die down. With how young Cal's sister was, and how ill his mother had become in the last few years, and how everything about their life had become so trying. I couldn't even try to imagine how difficult it all had been.

I had a feeling Cal had tried to tell me at least once, now that I thought back to all of our discussions. Of course he would have gotten around to it. He'd given me enough clues, after all. And there were so many other factors, more than even Miss Abernathy knew.

Like the fact that my father had known everything all along.

"Miss Abernathy, do you think he's still here…now?" I asked.

"Well, yes. His five thousand special gift donation was the first to be announced. Did you not hear? I'm sure he's still around. He would want to stay longer than to simply impress everyone with his generosity; he's likely here to declare to the world that he's back in Boston with plans to move into Hilldreth Manor, with money to spare."

"Excuse me then." I put my hand on Miss Abernathy's plump arm. "I was on my way up to the stage. I'd forgotten I wanted to tell them to announce my special gift donation as anonymous."

Honestly, they could have already announced it, and I wouldn't have known. I'd been so focused on everything Miss Abernathy had been willing to share in the last ten minutes.

"Why ever would you want to do that?" Miss Abernathy asked, incredulous. Then she seemed to understand my real cause in leaving so quickly, for she said, "Now, Nicholette, you don't mean to have an introduction made, do you? What are you thinking?"

But I'd already started for the other side of the room by the time she'd asked this. Which was just as well, because I didn't know what to think, except that I just needed to see *him*.

15

Mr. Hawthorne

"Thou hast ravished my heart."
— Song of Solomon 4:9

Searching the ballroom the best I could, I quickly examined every crowded group as I passed. Was Cal even there anymore? He'd told me he wouldn't be there, that he needed to keep a low profile. But then why had he come?

To make his substantial donation and reveal himself to Boston? Because he was eager to have his old—his *real* life back?

Because the case was over?

Or because he knew I'd be there?

As I circled the ballroom again, I had to admit that I might have missed him. Perhaps Cal had only come to make his monetary donation for the sake of the Children's Aid Society, and then left, not wanting me to see him. Realizing that I probably looked a bit ridiculous hurrying about the room as I was, I decided to find a quiet place to rest...to think.

There were all kinds of little corners and alcoves in the Cravens' third-floor ballroom, and I crept into one of the draped-off rooms, hoping no one else had had the same idea. There were five tall, rounded windows circling the turret-shaped room, all without curtains, all gathering moonlight and spreading it all about the floor. There was a small sofa and two chairs, as if the room were made for a tiny meeting area. I didn't know what else anyone would find to do in such a room during a ball…besides what I'd done in a very similar room at Everthorne…the last time I'd seen Cal.

Or rather, the last time I'd seen Chauncey Hawthorne III.

When he'd kissed me breathless.

I sat upon the sofa, turned to face the windows, and stared up at the full moon shining down into the little room.

God, is this You…? Is this You helping me?

I felt as though my whole world had shifted irreparably. And what would be left? I was in love with Cal…I knew this. But what would I do now? Would I be allowed to marry him? I wanted to. I still wanted to.

Instead of circling the ballroom aimlessly, I realized I should have simply found my father…but would his answers to my questions have been the same as they had been the last time I'd asked? Would he again simply tell me to go straight to the source, to get my answers from Cal?

It had been my goal, in searching the ballroom, not that I had planned what I'd say when I saw him.

The light-bluish drapes at the entrance to the little room rustled, and a burst of laughter came from the other side. Standing, thinking I should allow the room to the group of friends ready to escape the crowd—and not to just sit there and dither endlessly—I hurried toward the opening in order to leave. I reached the curtain just as it was pulled aside to reveal no group of friends, but only Cal Hawthorne.

He stepped into the little room, letting the blue curtain fall behind him. "Were you looking for someone?"

"Just you," I admitted. Not knowing how to feel besides utterly confused and completely and irresistibly drawn to him, I stayed my ground, right there in front of him, with maybe only a foot between us.

"I had hoped not to create too big a stir tonight." Cal didn't move, simply stared down at me as he spoke.

"Oh, but there is a stir," I muttered. Throughout the crowd, and also deep in my heart.

"I suppose I shouldn't be surprised. And something tells me you've already solved the mystery...of who I am."

I took a step back, still so very unprepared for what to say to him. I had so many questions, and not a word would come. And I didn't want to call him Chauncey. I could barely reconcile in my mind yet that he *was* Chauncey. However, the only thing that ending up coming out of my mouth as I looked into his familiar gray-blue eyes was, "You're...you're Chauncey O'Callaghan Hawthorne III."

"I told you my name could be considered atrocious." He came farther into the small room, taking up so much of the space with his impressive form. And yet, he seemed a bit shy now...as if he weren't quite sure of my response. "It's not exactly something one has practice admitting. Think how it would have sounded if I'd simply blurted it out, as I've been half-tempted to do a number of times."

"You could have simply told me your given name was Chauncey when I asked you last week at Everthorne." I thought of everything we'd said and done the last time we'd seen each other...and how differently I'd imagined this next meeting would be. "It probably would have been a good opportunity, considering everything else from later on that evening."

His stature was so tall and strong, so intimidatingly attractive as he stood before me. And for all his charm and rugged appeal, he still seemed unsure, and quite nervous. "Were you ready to hear it that night at Everthorne?"

"I was barely ready tonight." My words came out as a hoarse whisper.

"And would it have mattered then, Nicholette?" He closed the distance between us and inched his face closer to mine, also barely whispering the words. "Does it matter now?"

"Yes. Or no…well, actually, it would have…it might have. I'm glad you didn't tell me." I knew I'd come full circle; that nothing I'd just said made any sense. But really, little was making sense to me about anything. Except the fact that I still loved him, no matter what his name was.

"You're glad I didn't tell you."

"Ironically, it's probably best that I didn't know…best that I hadn't met you under the impression that Miss Claudine Abernathy has been trying to engrain in me tonight." Stepping back again, I bumped into one of the armchairs and fell into its seat. I sat up nervously, and he came forward and took my hand in his.

He lifted me to my feet but then refused to let go of my hand. Clasping it in his, he pressed it to his chest, over his heart. He took a step, and at the same instant, pulled me closer.

And I wasn't going to fight it any longer. There was no use. I knew the only place for me, truly, was with him, in his arms.

"This Mr. Chauncey Hawthorne III seems to have scandalized the gentile crowd gathered for this charity event, simply by showing up…and flaunting his money," I said.

"Now, now, I wouldn't say that…not if it's for a good cause. Consider my appearance tonight merely an opportunity to announce my family's return to Boston."

I turned my hand and gripped his, my fingers entwined between his…and he let out a deep breath, as if relieved. "I can understand that, but Miss Abernathy is positively beside herself. I don't know what she's going to do when she—"

"Yes, I recall her opinion from the dinner party last week. Is that what you are afraid of? That Miss Abernathy and her scandalized sentiments about my father are going to prevent us from being together?"

I lifted a hand to the sleeve of his jacket and combed my fingernails against the material, from his shoulder to his chest. Tugging gently at his lapel, I brought his face down to mine and said, "Don't you think that they—?"

"Not with everyone we have behind us. You just wait and see." Wrapping his other arm farther around my waist, he brought me closer, allowing his hand to come up behind my back and his fingers to rest on my bare shoulder. "Between your father, Bram Everstone—and especially when Miss Abernathy realizes that Charlotte Hawthorne is her dearest, favorite friend Letty Hawthorne, she'll come around."

Although his face was slowly nearing mine, and I knew very well that he was now much more interested in kissing me than talking, I couldn't help but ask, "Does this mean Ezra Hawthorne has been caught? That the case is over?"

"Yes, he's been apprehended and jailed. It happened the night of the dinner party at Everthorne, in fact."

"I'd had a feeling the urgent message was regarding your cousin, and I prayed for you, as I said I would."

"And I believe God answered those prayers." He lowered his head again, his gaze breaking from mine for the first time since he'd put his arms around me. Now, his eyes were focused on my lips. "And so many others besides."

"And now we can have our meeting with Dr. Wellesley?" I asked breathlessly.

He smiled. "It's already planned, and he's looking forward to it."

"Does Violet know about your true identity?" I asked, now merely flirting with his patience.

"She didn't until earlier today. My father had been estranged from her father since they were young, before any of us were born. Mother had always—in the somewhat irregular letters between my mother and hers—referred to me as Cal and Maybelle as Mabel, our long-time nicknames." He slid his fingers up to my cheek and then cradled my jaw in the palm of his hand. "But please don't mention anything about Ezra to Violet yet. She doesn't know that he'll likely hang for all he's done over the last few years. Although he's been entirely wicked, he *is* her brother."

"And now that it is finished, you're not going to help with anything else...very dangerous, are you?"

"I can't promise that I won't. As a Christian, I can only promise to follow where God leads...however, I don't see anything dangerous on the horizon."

"I see." But I understood his noble stance. It was part of who he was, and something about him that garnered even more admiration. "So what happened?" I asked.

"Nothing terrible, but it was definitely clear that God had His hand in the situation. But I've seen His hand work in so many other ways lately, it shouldn't have surprised me. God is the One who has made all of this possible." His cheek grazed mine, and he whispered, "When there seemed to be no way."

"For so many reasons," I reiterated, quietly. For it was definitely the truth.

"When I met you in the bookshop, I had my plan..." he said quietly. "That I would stay out of sight and not pursue you until the case was resolved, and I would be free to do so without secrets and misunderstandings..." He chuckled under his breath and stood back a bit, bringing his balled fist to his lips as he cleared his throat. Catching my eye again with an irresistible smile, he added, "At least that was my plan until I found you listening, waiting behind my bedchamber door that day Mabel sneaked you into my house."

My hand, which had been at his chest, slipped up his jacket to his shoulder. "I thought I wouldn't be blamed for that."

"It is true, I don't blame you…it's just that I haven't been able to get that image of you standing there out of my mind, no matter how I've tried." His arm tightened about my waist.

"Yes, I know the feeling." Though I'd meant my every thought of him over the last few months, from every moment I'd shared with him, I realized what I'd said had unfortunately sounded more specific to that one embarrassing instance.

"You also have trouble nixing that thought from your memory, Nicholette?"

I chose not to respond, considering the blush I could already feel creeping into my cheeks was incriminating enough.

"So I decided I wouldn't lose you again—no matter the case, no matter the fact that you couldn't know my real name because of the case, and no matter that we had no idea when we'd actually nab Ezra."

"And Father encouraged you, didn't he?"

"It was some time after our meeting in the bookshop that he first visited me at Rochester Farms and admitted he'd figured out why I'd left the bank years ago—because of what my father had done."

"He would hardly tell me anything about you," I admitted. "Except that it pleased him to have me know you."

"I begged him not to tell you my true identity, under the guise that it was more for the sake of letting the rumors settle a bit more. He didn't understand, of course, that it was because of my involvement with the police we'd not made the transition. No one was supposed to know our true identities while I was undercover, you see. Least of all you."

At this, Cal sat us upon the sofa, his arm still about my waist, and both of mine still draped around his shoulders.

"He was quite eager to see how things would progress between us, for he was fearful you would become too interested in a certain Mr. Alexander Summercourt to give me a decent chance." An irresistible smirk graced his lips, his dimples coming out full force with the glee-filled smile. I couldn't help it. I pulled him down to me and kissed him.

One arm remained looped around me, and the other was now braced against the wooden back of the high sofa, as if he weren't certain whether to allow the kiss to go on or not. And then he pulled away, but only an inch—with a mere inch between our faces, he said, "Well, we know where that particular gentleman stands now."

"He never had a chance with you around." I sighed against his chest, happily.

Cal took his hand from the sofa and brought it around my shoulders. "I knew if I could make you love me, despite everything, then perhaps it wouldn't matter so much when you found out about my father, and realized the stigma that came with my name."

I sat back, put a few more inches between us, and studied his face, knowing he was being quite serious now, speaking of his father.

"You know, even after I'd learned that William had been killed, I thought I'd come to the point of being content to let you go. I thought, because of what my father had done, with my being stripped of my inheritance and having to work at Rochester Farms, I'd never have another chance with you."

"But your Great Uncle Perceval."

"Yes, while you were still in Europe last spring, my father's Uncle Percy had fallen deathly ill. He'd never married himself, had no children...and so, in his will, bestowed everything he had to us, increasing our wealth by a tenfold compared to what we received from my father."

"Why did you keep working for Mr. Rochester long into the summer?—and why work for my father?"

"Because I needed to keep up appearances with Ezra, and because I loved working at the bank with your father. And then there's May... I'll likely need to produce quite the dowry for her..." Cal laughed under his breath. "In order to induce someone to marry her."

"Oh, she isn't so terrible as that." I hugged him closer.

"Possibly." He shrugged. "Perhaps with a bit of guidance from you, she'll make a fine match...without the need of bribery."

"I'd heard that your father's name was Robert," I dared to ask with a low voice. "How is that?"

"In the same way my name is Cal, he'd chosen the name as a boy when everyone confused him with his father."

"Then why are you called Cal, and not Chauncey?"

"Because no one wants to be called Chauncey." He gave me his amazing half-grin that had so brilliantly captivated my attention all those months before.

"So when I met you years ago, it was as Chauncey Hawthorne III, and not Cal Hawthorne, wasn't it?"

"Correct."

"I still don't remember meeting you... just that name."

"That doesn't surprise me." He smiled down at me again, but this time in self-depreciation. "Apparently, I wasn't very memorable back then."

"Well, you are now."

"I had so many doubts. I didn't know how you'd react to the muddle my life had become."

From listening to Miss Abernathy's judgments upon the "disgraced Hawthorne family" a half hour before, I could easily imagine the difficult time it had been for him, his mother, and Mabel to live through. And my heart only went out to them.

"Apparently, I don't mind the muddle." After a few seconds, I continued. "From the moment we met at Brittle Brattle Books, Cal

Hawthorne, you've had me turned inside out." I clutched the lapels of his jacket and stared into his blue eyes. "You've invaded my life, enchanted my heart, my very soul. I had no defenses, and there is now no way I can stop."

As this registered, his gaze lingered, and he remained quiet for some moments. "Then you'll forgive me for being such a mystery— for keeping you in the dark about so many things?"

"Of course." I laughed. "Just no more secrets, all right? You can tell me anything, always, and I'd like you to start with answering one last question I have."

"And what is that?"

"Why have you purchased Hilldreth Manor from Nathan and Amaryllis Everstone?"

"Oh that…" He looked away, shyly, though we were still very much in each other's arms. "It's just that lately, I've been strongly considering the idea of getting married again."

I pulled his lapels again, bringing his gaze back to meet mine. "Is that a fact?"

"I thought any new bride would want a home to call her own, and it seemed like a nice house…one she would like."

"And may I ask, who the fortunate young lady is?"

"You, silly. If you'll have me."

"Hmm…" I stalled playfully. But I didn't take my eyes from his, nor did I let him go. "I think I will have to, Mr. Chauncey Hawthorne III, for I fear I am desperately in love with you."

"Good, because I feel quite the same." Cal took his arms from around me and stood, taking my hand as he helped me to my feet. "Now, why don't we find your parents and do what we can to shock Miss Abernathy by making our happy announcement?" He placed his hand over mine and caught my eye as he guided me out of the curtained-off room, out to the crowds. "But first, Mrs. Everstone, I do hope you know how to waltz."

"But of course."

Ignoring the groups of people congregated about, Cal pushed through them, pulling me along. When we reached the open floor, he took my hand in his, extended our grasped hands, and then wrapped his arm around my waist. I sank into his embrace, delighted by the feel of his arms about me again. I hadn't danced in years, and never with anyone able to make my entire body hum with anticipation, the way he did.

We joined the dancers waltzing to "The Fairy Wedding Waltz" the orchestra played at the other end of the ballroom, and for a few moments we were silent, simply relishing being in each other's arms, with so much to look forward to in our future together. Then, as his blue eyes took on a new gleam, he said, "I just realized you haven't told me your given name. You know mine now—what's yours?"

"Oh, right." I leaned back against his hand at my waist and glanced down, a bit embarrassed.

"I do think if I'm going to marry you, I should have the privilege of knowing what it is. We had a deal, remember?"

"My first name is Guinevere. I was named for my mother, and then Nicholette is for my father."

"Guinevere Nicholette Fairbanks Everstone? It is beautiful. Just as you are."

"No, it's about as atrocious as Chauncey O'Callaghan Hawthorne III."

"Our names are well-matched." Cal tugged me closer, near enough that his breath tickled my hair as he whispered, "But I must admit, adding 'Hawthorne' to the end of your name, very soon, *will* improve your name, and a great many other things, besides."

Immensely glad to hear his opinion concerning the projected length of our engagement, I smiled and caught his gaze, matching gleam for gleam. "Yes, I do believe it will, Mr. Hawthorne. Very, very soon."

EPILOGUE

Five Weeks Later

"A wonderful fact to reflect upon,
that every human creature is constituted to be that profound
secret and mystery to every other."
—Charles Dickens, *A Tale of Two Cities*

Saturday, September 23, 1893 · Laurelton, Maine

I've always heard mention of Everston, since it was close to where Violet resided most of her life," Mabel said cheerfully. She sat beside her mother, across from me and Cal, in our rented carriage from Severville, Maine, where the train line from Boston had ended. "I never imagined it would take almost half a day to get here. What was the town called, Mother? And how much farther is it to Blakeley House?"

"Westward, dear," said Mrs. Charlotte Hawthorne, my new mother-in-law. "I don't think it is far from here. It certainly is a trip, though not so long that you can't easily take the train up and visit me a few times a year."

"Yes, of course I will, Mother....So the town of Westward, that is where the Hawthorne Inn was located?" Mabel winked at me and gave Cal a sly grin. "Is that correct?"

"Yes, May." Cal gave his sister a rather harsh look and tightened his arm around my shoulders.

I could just imagine what Mabel was thinking, knowing her penchant for adventure. I was sure she would try to find a way to get there in the next two weeks so she could snoop around the house, which was currently abandoned.

"But now that Ezra's been put in jail and his *business pursuits* have been put to an end, Violet has regained ownership of the Hawthorne Inn," Cal told her pointedly. "I think she and Vance are planning to turn it into a summer home away from Boston. And we *won't* be going there until it's finished."

"Oh! How glorious!" Mabel responded snidely, knowing she'd been caught.

"The poor old house…" I said softly, turning to Cal, for I could not imagine going back to a house so terribly misused in my absence.

"I know what you mean, but don't worry," he reassured me. "There have been a great number of prayers said in and over that house, and I'm sure the Lord will bless the time Violet and Vance spend there, despite what's been going on within the walls in recent years."

My mother-in-law sighed, staring out the window. "Let's speak of something more edifying." She turned her sad, gray eyes to Cal and slowly revealed a little smile. "I cannot wait to see Claudine again. I'm glad she was able to quickly move out of Hilldreth so you two could marry and live there for a little while before helping me move to Everston to join her."

I was also glad for the last three weeks, living at Hilldreth Manor…married to Cal…feeling so intensely, immensely over the moon. Something about having the house all to myself—and Cal—was invigorating when it came to "going home." I'd been inside that house a thousand times over the course of my life, but never had I imagined that I'd feel the most complete happiness I'd ever known within those walls.

And I was also happy that with a little help from me, Mother Charlotte had persuaded her two children to let her live year-round at Everston near her good friend, Miss Claudine Abernathy. Dexter and Estella had basically given Miss Abernathy their newly remodeled apartment on the top floor of the six-story tower of rooms when they'd had their new house built over the summer. But of course, Cal's mother wasn't about to let them do the same for her, when she had plenty of funds to pay them for her room and board at the elegant resort. She would be living in one of the smaller apartments on the ground floor. She and Miss Abernathy could enjoy a life of peace and tranquility, without anyone expecting anything from them, as would have been the case had they remained in Boston.

"It's a wonder that Estella ended up married to the new owner of Everston when her father sold it a few years back," I said, trying to keep the conversation light, as we would soon arrive at Estella's newly built Blakeley House. "I'm not certain how it happened, but from what I've gathered, it was most definitely a love match."

"Well, good for them," Mother Charlotte commented. "That is the very best kind."

I glanced down bashfully. It pained me to think from whence her kind words had come—for she'd definitely not had the fortune of marrying for love herself and then had gone through so much misery because the harsh betrayal Cal's father had put them through when he'd died.

Yet there she was, smiling and so happy for us and our marital bliss.

"I'm happy for her," I said. "The last I knew, she was sick in love with someone who wouldn't have her. He wanted to be a missionary and didn't think she'd suit."

"How tragic!" I looked up just in time to see Mabel's worried gaze dart from Cal and me to her mother. Which was odd. Mabel had never mentioned anything about having a specific interest in any one gentleman. What would make her so melancholy at the mention of such rejection?

"Yes, well, only if you look at the situation from her perspective years ago," I reassured her. "I think Estella would say she's very happy with the way things have turned out. She has Dexter and Gracie, and now baby Kent...and all this—" With an outstretched hand, I directed Mabel's gaze to the open carriage window which, at that moment, revealed a long lake surrounded by pine and white-barked birch trees. Just above the treetops, a red roof came into view—the top story of the resort and Miss Abernathy's new home. "We're getting close to Everston now. Look."

As all four of us gazed out the windows, even more of the impressive hotel came into view.

"It's too bad we're expected to go straight to Blakeley House first," Mabel said with a little more composure. "I was looking forward to riding the elevator at Everston." She tapped her fingers impatiently against the clasp of her reticule.

"There will be plenty of time to explore the resort, Mabel," her mother replied. "You'll have two weeks, after all, until you'll return to Boston with Violet. I doubt that you'll be expected much at the house once the party is finished today. Not with the new little one for them to care for. I must say, two babies in a year is quite a feat for your dear friend, Nicholette. Isn't Estella's first child not yet a year old?"

"Gracie will be a year old in a few weeks."

"And your old friend Meredyth will be there at Blakeley House when we arrive, won't she, Nick?" Cal asked, purposefully removing the topic of newborn infants from the conversation. Although his mother was moving to Maine and we would likely only see her a few times a year, he knew from the short period he'd been married to Alice that we would soon be badgered about when our own children would make an appearance.

Although the idea wasn't a terrible one to dwell upon, and I looked forward to the day I'd become a mother, Cal and I certainly did enjoy that we had Hilldreth Manor to ourselves. After all, we were newly wed.

Before I was even able to answer Cal's question about Meredyth, the long gravel, forested road we'd been traveling upon turned into a narrow lane, a virtual tunnel of trees, and we came upon an impressive limestone house. And there, on the porch watching for us, were Meredyth Hampton and Amaryllis Everstone. It had been almost two and a half years since I'd seen either of them—at my wedding to William. Amaryllis looked much the same, but Meredyth was most definitely with child.

As the carriage came to a halt, more of my old friends joined them on the porch and I realized what a great number of people were in on this surprise get-together for Bram Everstone. Of course, Nathan was there with Amaryllis and Lawry Hampton, Meredyth's long-time best friend and now husband, all stood on the porch. Nathan's twin sister, Natalia, and her husband, George Livingston, came down the steps with Estella and Dexter Blakeley, whose house everyone had apparently invaded.

The only people who seemed to be missing—besides Bram and his wife, Evangeline—were Vance, Violet, and Miss Abernathy. They had been tasked with getting my former father-in-law and his wife from Everston to Blakeley House at a certain time.

Since Cal and I had mostly kept a low profile throughout our very short engagement—and then even more so while secluding ourselves in our wonderful Hilldreth Manor, with only the exception of having his mother and sister over for dinner every other evening—I was not prepared for the hail of celebratory comments from everyone as we alighted the carriage. Oh, yes, it certainly was difficult to remember the time I wasn't Cal's wife. I'd felt that my place beside him had been established for ages, not a mere three weeks.

I bowed my head shyly and clutched Cal's hand, unused to the compliments from these friends of mine, half of whom I'd known my entire life…and should have been related to, if not for William's accidental death.

But Cal.

I glanced up to my husband of three weeks, taking in his gorgeous smile as he greeted everyone with ease, completely in awe of what we'd become, and how, together, we seemed to fit perfectly into this circle of friends I'd known forever.

Dexter went to the wide front door and held it open. "Now, do let's all get back into the house, for they will be here any minute."

As I turned to follow the others in, Estella came up beside me and then took my arm in hers as we walked through the doorway. "I'm so glad you and your Mr. Hawthorne were able to make it, but there's barely time to spare. I hope they didn't spot your carriage on the road past Everston."

"I think our rented carriage is inconspicuous enough," I reassured her. "They shouldn't have thought anything of it."

"I hope not. We've been planning this weekend for months. Even before we knew there was a possibility that you'd ever be married to Violet's cousin." Estella gave me a sly grin. "My, I thought I'd had a hurried engagement! But it does seem that it's the best thing to do once your love is sure. There's no use waiting after that."

I hugged her. "No, there isn't."

Her large stone house was decorated with a very English look, very much like the castle that it resembled from the outside. There were two main rooms off the front hall, and Estella and Dexter guided everyone into them, so there were a few of us on each side of the hall. Fortunately, Cal had followed Estella and me into the parlor to the left, with Amaryllis, Nathan, my mother-in-law, and Mabel.

"This family of Vance's takes some getting used to," Cal whispered to me with a slight grin. "Not that it surprises me...now that I think about it."

I thought it odd that he would think of the Everstone family as "Vance's family," but then I realized that's how he'd first come in contact with them. And Vance had been the one whom he'd befriended, first and foremost.

Vance. I was beginning to forgive him...slowly. He was one of Cal's best friends now and I knew we would be spending much time together in the future, so there were multiple reasons I needed to keep trying. It wasn't as difficult to visit Everthorne anymore, now that I'd had a chance to heal from the pain of losing the life I'd looked forward to having with William, and especially since I'd fallen in love with Cal...but still.

Vance was such a conundrum. He had reconciled with his family when he'd married Violet and moved in down the street from his father instead of running all around Europe evading him. Vance definitely wasn't the same man who'd caused so much grief for everyone when he'd thoughtlessly brought the danger from his past full force to my wedding with William. Somehow, I had to forgive him for that.

Estella drew back the curtains at the front window. "The carriage is here—they're almost up to the porch!" Her excitement about this surprise party for her father made my heart swell and a smile form upon my lips. This really was a great and wonderful family. When was the last time that Bram Everstone had seen all of his living children together? At Estella's wedding almost two years before?

What a surprise for him, indeed.

When the butler drew open the door, he welcomed them in, as normally as possible, I supposed, and then as Bram Everstone, his wife, Vance, Violet, and Miss Abernathy all walked into the entryway, Estella stepped past the threshold and apparently could do nothing save wrap her arms around her father and hug him. A moment later, the rest of us from the two front parlors joined them in the hall and Bram Everstone's surprise at seeing everyone there took its effect.

"My, what a crowd!"

"It's all for you, Father. We thought you'd enjoy seeing more than just your newest grandchild."

"And you couldn't have been more right, daughter."

After the party settled down a bit, everyone congregated into one of the parlors and sat around the long spacious room. Cal and I sat in the far corner with his mother and Miss Abernathy, giving the Everstones their space as they talked, visited, and cooed over the grandchildren, including Estella's newborn.

Wishing we'd made it to Blakeley House with time to relax after our ten-hour journey from Boston, I couldn't help but rest my head upon Cal's shoulder. "What it must be like to travel from Boston to Severville in the comfort of your own Pullman rail car… Bram and Evangeline look as fresh as I felt this morning when boarding."

Cal leaned in and whispered smartly, "They also had a little time at Everston before joining us here."

I turned my head, the edge of his jaw at my brow. "We should have come up yesterday. I probably look a fright from our long journey today."

"Not true. You look perfectly wonderful." He brought a finger up to my neck and caressed the back of my ear. "Delectably scrumptious, in fact."

Smiling, I looked up and noticed a maid walk into the room from the farthest entrance, rolling a cart with what looked like a chocolate cake…with candles?

Violet stood from her seat with Mabel and took Vance by the hand, leading him to the cake. The rest of the guests stood then as well, Cal and I included, and gathered at the other end of the room around the cart.

Dexter stood between everyone and the cake, holding his newborn son. "Now, it just happens that baby Kent came along just in time to celebrate someone else's birthday as well." He held his hand out to his brother-in-law. "Vance turns twenty-nine today."

Before Vance could reply, Bram Everstone started in with the first words to the tune, "For He's a Jolly Good Fellow," and everyone else immediately joined in, singing the song in Vance's honor.

Again, I marveled at how God had made a place for him, this black sheep of the Everstones—this prodigal son come home—who was evidently still so loved by his family, despite everything he'd put them through over the years.

Cal took my hand as we stood behind the crowd of the family that had almost been mine...and still sort of was. He feathered his fingers over my palm, catching my attention, and my gaze. I breathed one word, "What?"

"We are blessed, indeed, with such friends."

"Indeed."

Once the song was finished, Vance faced everyone unabashedly, looking as if he'd taken the stage and had something important to say. "Well, that was entirely uncalled for...but since you're all here and waiting for me to say something..." He looked to Violet for a moment and she smiled, so he continued. "I will say something. Violet informed me yesterday that in about six months, she's going to have a baby."

After this momentous news, there really was no stopping the hustle and bustle in the room as everyone shared their congratulatory remarks. With the excitement of such wonderful things to come, the joy was contagious.

Looking across the long room, I noticed both Miss Abernathy and my mother-in-law slumped over in the two armchairs in the corner, fast asleep. Well, at least they were getting their rest. And Mabel and Violet were chatting boisterously with Amaryllis and Meredyth as they all got to know each other better.

"Goodness," I whispered to Cal. "All these people…and the busyness…I honestly don't think we've been in such a crowd more than once, and that was at the Charity Ball last month. Which absolutely seems as though it were a thousand years ago. So many things have changed since that night."

My husband of three weeks took a step forward, an irresistible little smirk upon his lips. "The best of all is the fact that you're now all mine."

"Oh, I don't know. Perhaps it's more that *you're* now all *mine*."

"We could debate…or we could simply excuse ourselves to the balcony over there…" Cal nodded toward the double leaded glass doors at the center of the room. "We could endeavor to reconcile our differences, as I have a very good idea about just how to do that…"

I playfully elbowed Cal in the side, smiling most giddily, a little embarrassed that someone in the room might overhear him say such silly things.

Cal's expression suddenly turned thoughtful. "We could also discuss a few other possibilities regarding spending more time up here near Everston. It is gorgeous up here—and we'd be close to Mother, not to mention Vance, Violet, Estella, and Dexter."

"Do you mean move up here—build a house of our own?"

"For the summers, at least. Or we could simply live at Everston for a few months a year. Summers here are said to be quite pleasant. What do you think?"

Astonished by this sudden and very welcome idea, I could only stare at him and let out a little half-laugh. I took a few steps closer to the windows along the wall next to the doors leading out to the balcony, looking at the woods and mountains surrounding Blakeley House with new eyes. Cal followed me, taking my hand again as he opened the door and quietly led me outside.

"What do you think?" he asked again as he closed the door behind us.

"I think it would be...marvelous."

"Marvelous, yes, but I'm not so certain how much May will love the idea. She may want to remain in Boston; I can't see her relishing having to spend an entire summer in the country, even with the crowds Everston would provide. It was difficult enough trying to get her to come up for the next two weeks."

"We could have her stay the summer with someone... like Sylvie is right now. They both have lots of friends who would love to have them for a summer."

"Well, then, the plans are set." The wind picked up just then, sending the long, loose blonde strands of my hair flowing in the breeze. Cal reached up and gathered them between his fingers and tucked them behind my ear. "Now, about what I said in there..." He gave a slight nod to the doors. "About reconciling our differences—"

Before he could say another thing, I put my arms around his neck, pulled him down to me, and kissed him.

After a few minutes, I pulled back. "You were right," I admitted breathlessly, with as much seriousness as I could muster.

Cal stared down at me, apparently a bit lost for words. "I was—I am?"

"I suppose I can allow you to be right—that my being yours is the best thing to happen in the last five weeks...as long as you promise to keep kissing me like that."

"I can most definitely keep that promise," he said softly with that enchanting smile of his. "For as long as you'd like, Mrs. Hawthorne."